PARAKEET

PARAKEET

MARIE-HELENE BERTINO

FARRAR, STRAUS AND GIROUX | NEW YORK

Farrar, Straus and Giroux
120 Broadway, New York 10271

Printed in the United States of America
First edition, 2020

Library of Congress Cataloging-in-Publication Data
Names: Bertino, Marie-Helene, author.
Title: Parakeet / Marie-Helene Bertino.
Description: First edition. | New York : Farrar, Straus and Giroux, 2020.
Identifiers: LCCN 2020003423 | ISBN 9780374229450 (hardcover)
Subjects: GSAFD: Mystery fiction. | Paranormal fiction.
Classification: LCC PS3602.E7683 P37 2020 | DDC 813/.6—dc23
LC record available at https://lccn.loc.gov/2020003423

Designed by Gretchen Achilles

Our books may be purchased in bulk for promotional, educational,
or business use. Please contact your local bookseller or the Macmillan
Corporate and Premium Sales Department at 1-800-221-7945, extension 5442,
or by e-mail at MacmillanSpecialMarkets@macmillan.com.

www.fsgbooks.com
www.twitter.com/fsgbooks • www.facebook.com/fsgbooks

1 3 5 7 9 10 8 6 4 2

For Thomas Everett Dodson

PARAKEET

One week before my wedding day, upon returning to my hotel room with a tube of borrowed toothpaste, I find a small bird waiting inside the area called the antechamber and know within moments it is my grandmother. I recognize the glittering, hematite eyes, the expression of cunning disapproval. The odor of a gym at close of day encircles her.

What is the Internet? the bird says, does not say.

Her head is the color of warning: sharp curve, yield-yellow. The eyes on either side of the Cro-Magnon crown are lined the way hers were in shoddy cornflower pencil as if to say, *Really look, here.* Her hair, that had throughout her life hurled silvery messages skyward, has been replaced by orderly, navy stripes that emanate down her pate like ripples in silk. Under the beak where her unpronounced chin would have been, four regal feathers pose, each marked by an ebony dot. She hovers inches above the sofa's back, chastened and restless by her new form.

The toothpaste lands with a dull thud on the carpet. I'm silent when stunned. No getting me to talk.

What is the Internet? my grandmother the bird insists, speaking as if we are in the middle of a conversation, which, in a way, we are.

She had called to ask this question ten years before. At the time I considered explaining the technological phenomenon, but she was so old. What would be the point, I reasoned, of telling her about the show priming to begin after her exit? There have been many times in my life when, encountering an opportunity to do good, for reasons of shyness or shock, an unwillingness to leave a safe perch has made me balk. I told my grandmother the Internet was solely for engineers and that its effect on society would be nominal.

The following day she climbed a ladder poised against her house, meaning to hammer a warped shingle. Something like a phone call—we were never certain—summoned her. She misremembered the ladder, fell from the roof, and lay unconscious until a neighbor found her. For a month we attempted to will her out of a coma with the music of Lawrence Welk. She preferred to stay asleep.

After she was gone, every room was a nothing room.

I don't regret letting others rush forward to care for strangers in need. I don't regret calling my brother a little shit on his wedding day. However, lying to my grandmother about the Internet placed a painful pebble at the bottom of my stomach that would not go away.

Now, my second chance claws the rim of a water glass in present, Internet-rich day, as alive as the rest of us, trying to sip through her beak and failing.

"It turned out to be more influential than I led you to believe," I say.

No shit.

Tasked with explaining it, I realize how little I know about the

Internet. "It began as numbers on a screen." I make a blurping
sound to signify dial-up and explain that it grew from a device
only a few people had, to Wi-Fi, which I think is in the air? I gesture to indicate: exploding. Network names showcase a defining
feature of the user. Biscottiworshipper. Sadoboegirl. "People
use it to promote themselves like brands." This is deep and rich
information. My cheeks heat, I'm proud of myself. I extrapo-
late: "Because everyone is famous, no one is." I deepen, reverse:
"Which is, like everything else, a good and bad thing." I say,
"Link, blog, router, spam."

Even as a bird my grandmother's dubiousness is unmistakable. The cocked avian focus, doubting me. When she was alive,
she preferred staying in her slippers all day and the term "shove it
up your ass" to anything, maybe even to my grandfather who over
time became a scudding, booted shadow in the house's secondary
rooms. In the garage, winding a clock. In the spare bedroom, re-
pairing an outlet. Shove the clock. Shove the outlet. If my grandmother ever regretted slicing into another's feelings like fondant,
she never admitted it. Any room containing her was merry. This
was a big deal for me, since most of my childhood felt panicked
and serious. She'd listen and move her eyebrows in a way that
corrected my perspective. With a gaze, she could lift me older.

Offended on behalf of the product I've just begun to understand, I sell. "There's almost no living being you can't connect
with."

At "no living being" I think of her, legs tucked into her plum-
age, "sitting" above the cushions. *How does it feel to be connected to
every living thing?*

"Sad," I admit, and she says, *Sad?*

"When you can see anyone at any hour, it collapses perspective and time. Add to that the isolation and distance from which

most people observe, and the Internet gives the impression that one person is simultaneously having a party, turning fifty, scuba diving, baking with a great aunt."

Sounds like a giant panic attack.

"That's not technology's fault," I say. "The Internet is indifferent. It's the people who ruin it, posting only highlights, like every night is Saturday night. But most of life is Wednesday afternoon, and no one thinks that's meaningful. They omit loneliness and tedium. The people who do post honestly are considered whiners."

The bird huffs, nods. *No one should bother anyone else with their problems.* This had been a phrase she used in life and one of the fueling philosophies of our family. *What a waste of time.*

"It is, but there are beautiful aspects to it." I press a few buttons on my phone to conjure a picture.

Goodie, she says. *A wall.*

"The Great Wall of China," I correct her. "Everyone can visit faraway places. Kind of. It's a grand leveler in terms of class."

If you can afford a phone, I guess.

I change the screen option and a grid of photographs appears. "People have their own page on their preferred platform." I scroll so she can see:

A frosted cake. Dog on a forest path. Woman smiling over macaroni. Page of a book. Pulled taffy. Boy mussed from a nap. Lit pool. Selfie of a woman balancing a cat on either shoulder. A dog eats Cheez-Its off pink linoleum. A sign: DO NOT SHELVE ITEMS IN AISLE THREE WITHOUT ASKING JOANNA. Bunting in a desert town. Aproned gelato server hovering over delicate, pastel vats.

"A good way to connect with what are called 'friends,'" I say. "Not regular friends, usually it's like the guy who plays softball with your coworker."

Who wants to be more connected? the bird says, does not say. *Everyone is friends now?*

"I think people dislike other people at the ratio they did before you—"

We're not going to get very far if you can't say died.

"It's called virtual." I frown. "I'm not describing this correctly."

You're describing it fine.

"How would you know?" I say at the same time as she says, *But how would I know?*

I've come a week early to this inn on the shaft of Long Island to prepare for the transition from woman to wife, to do what the groom calls "decompress" because "of late" I've become a bit of a "nightmare." To break apart if necessary, but to do so properly, amid slatted pool chairs and conference coffee. I'm thirty-six, ethnically ambiguous, and hold an intense job I do not like, biographer of people with traumatic brain injury. I present their lives in court, using storyboards and dioramas. Everyone is thrilled I'm getting married. No one can believe I've found such a sweet man. Everyone adores the treats sold in this town that are hybrids of bagels and flatbread. Flagels.

The Inn's website boasts a recent remodel, yet the old design has only been reinforced with fresh paint so it looks newly out of date. Above the mud-colored carpets, wallpaper vines strangle the walls, here and there resulting in a salmon-colored tulip. There are fleets of staircases and elevators and floors large enough to simultaneously host several cathartic events. In another banquet hall, another wedding will run alongside ours. The plural of catharsis is catharses. The turnover is quick. Already, a lobby poster welcomes attendees of the following week's conference that seems to be about technology and clouds.

The Inn is buckled to a famous lake that features prominently on the town's signage. None of my people are from this area so the lake is not famous to us. It is akin to pointing to an actor and saying, *That's so and so*, from a show we've never watched. A gazebo sits in an exultation of cattails. A ruffle of trash by the edge of one of the lake's many inlets. I prefer the ocean because it is ugly and secretive and moody and can growl. Mind you, I'm "awful" and "rarely satisfied."

So far, my relaxation has manifested in inventing needs so I can have lingering conversations with the staff. I was finishing the place cards earlier when I thought, toothpaste, and wandered downstairs to inquire about the photograph taped to the concierge's computer screen.

"I'm not sure if you're aware what day you've landed on." I speak to the bird in the grated voice you employ for a guest who's arrived too early. "It's Sunday. I'm getting married in six days." I gesture to the migration of folded cards that cover the carpet in ecru Vs, anointed with all I can recall from high school calligraphy. "I have a work appointment tomorrow, a meeting with the florist, then I host our families for the groom's dinner. Mom, stepfather, friends arrive later this week. Et cetera. Have you come to wish me well?" I say, but knowing her, my tone contains no hope.

Of course I know you're getting married. The edges of her projection spit and haw. *Do you think I'm here to ask about wires in a box?* She goes transparent and her skeleton shows blinding bright, then whatever debatably divine force is conjuring her regains composure and she is opaque again. *There's something I want you to do.*

A rap on the door startles me and the bird, who fwips from the glass to the table like traveling from one thought to the next.

Through the peephole, I see a bellboy standing above a rolling table holding a metal-covered plate. "Ma'am?"

"I didn't order anything," I say.

Several feet behind him, the elevator dings. He says, "It's a surprise."

My grandmother warbles.

"Surprise!" He is faux cheerful.

I open the door. He glides in, activates the brakes on each table leg, flips the plate's cover to reveal a cake that says, *Congratulations!*, bats a napkin he pulls from an unseen compartment against the air then folds it into a triangle. His expression grows concerned, echoing mine.

I have what people call an out-loud face, one that others mimic without realizing. It may be the generous, peat-colored eyebrows, or the phrase they make with my conversation-piece nose. Strangers ask, *Are you confused?* Or, comment: *You're having fun.* What they mean is, I'm less good than others at hiding.

The bellboy follows my gaze to the grandmother now roosted on the pillow and shrieks, drops the napkin. "A bird!" He heads to the door. "I'll get the manager."

"No need to call anyone," I say. "It's handled."

"I hate birds," he says. "Like, really hate."

My grandmother's feathers shiver with laughter.

"She's very small," I bargain.

"Doesn't matter," he says. "Small, big. Hate them and always have."

My grandmother flies across the room and clings to the frame of a painting with one mirthful claw. This enjoyment of other people's discomfort was true in life. She is at once wholly grandmother and wholly bird, as she produces a multigarble that sounds like bland women kvetching. Louder, then louder.

"Oh god," he says. "What's it doing?" His fear is so antic it must be a put-on. He cowers in a crescent shape against the wall.

Tack, tack, my grandmother threatens cheerfully.

"I'm calling the concierge," he whispers.

"Stop," I tell her. Then to him, "We don't need the concierge. This is my bird. We were talking."

"'My'?" he says. "'Talking'?"

"Birds talk," I say.

My grandmother seems to chitchat with herself then produces a showy, wooden, *Hello.*

I imagine the room from his perspective. Bride talking to bird. He looks like a kid who muscles through situations in which women want him to leave with what he thinks is charm. But he's probably never met women like us. Critical, exuding a very taken vibe, hawkish (on certain evenings literally). Even in bird form my grandmother is all of these things, you can tell by the way she's needling him with gleeful, haughty eyes.

"Money." I hand him a twenty. "Don't tell the concierge I have a bird in here."

He winces, consults the bill in his hand.

"Secret," I say. And, in case it's the kind of thing that matters to him: "I'm the bride."

I guide him out. "Thank you for the surprise," I say. "I do like sweets."

"Raspberry." His voice is sad.

I want to seal the transaction with a compliment. "This is one of the nicest places I've ever stayed in Long Island." Not technically a lie. I've never stayed anywhere else.

"On." He snaps to attention. "Long Island. We say *on*."

"On Long Island?" I test. "Does that make sense?"

He nods. "On."

I close the door and return to the antechamber where the bird is sitting mid-cake. *Give an old lady a break*, she says, does not say. *I can't have any fun?*

She tries for a raspberry but neither berry nor beak will allow her to eat. She exists in this world but can exert no physical influence, which is news to someone like her.

Her mother, my great-grandmother, was banished from the Basque Country for getting pregnant with a Romany's child. She missed the banishing ship she was supposed to take from France to America. I like to think it was because she lost track of time while doing her hair. You never know what worse luck your bad luck saved you from. It was 1912. The ship she was supposed to take was the *Titanic*. Fig, I missed my ship. Sound of ship hitting an iceberg. Sound of ship cracking in half. Sound of cello. The scuffle of drowning. Safely on another vessel two days behind the *Titanic*, my great-grandmother gazed across the icy churn, my grandmother growing in her like an amniotic orchid, an accidental immigrant. My grandmother was tormented in her white neighborhood for her dark skin, and carried that pain into adulthood, where it bloomed into benevolent disgust. She gave birth to an ice chip, my mother.

Years later on the pale disk of Lake Champlain, my mother missed a ferry. In the hour she spent waiting for the next one she drank a Seven and Seven and met my father, a dockworker from the mountains who was the first in his family to cross a state line. He died of heart failure when my brother and I were young, leaving us alone with her temper, a line of crystal in igneous rock. A secret to everyone except those who lived with her.

Missing boats is a family trait.

Fun with the bellboy abandoned, the bird turns to business. *Is he tall?*

I know she means the groom. "No."

Does he have all his hair?

"It is in fact his distinguishing characteristic." I tell her he is an elementary school principal who coaches basketball, plays guitar, and sings to second graders about the solar system. Everyone loves the planet song.

Show me a picture.

I scroll down my personal web page, but there is only one picture of a tree at dusk. "I keep meaning to add more." Searching my phone, I find a picture of him holding three basketballs, the straps of several duffels hoisted over his shoulder. *Oh*, she says. *He's white.*

"We're white," I say.

She says, *Kind of.*

"We're considered white now," I say, insulted that she hasn't mentioned his clear green eyes, or, like, his ability to carry several things at once. ". . . the world is run by computers, and you're a bird. Not to beat a dead horse."

She is frustrated with me but will say what she has come to say. More of an understanding with space than movement, she intuits from table edge to sofa back. She lifts her beak as to achieve a silent auditorium a composer raises his wand.

What I want you to do is find your brother.

Of course, I already know. Knew before she asked about the

Internet, knew before rounding the corner to the antechamber and finding a judgmental budgie, perhaps even before, when I— balancing my room key, wallet, phone, and toothpaste—reached the door and realized I had no way of opening it and had to place each item on the ground, turn the knob, collect them again, all the while a turbulence spreading beneath my breastplate, which contained the maddening carbonation that could signal only one person. Tom. The thrilling dread that precedes his presence perhaps his only reliable quality. As kids, we slept pressed together like deer. The type of brother who will be your plus one to the play party or log roll, extol the virtues of heroin so lovingly you cry, clear dawn's crust from your windshield, but will not have brunch with you, or meet your best friend, or join you on the errand, or even answer his phone. The image I summon when thinking of him is akin to a certain laughing trouble. Any conflict I've ever encountered—and any alchemy—the tendency the world has to upend: unexpected money, a pretty line of stray cats, a bird-shaped grandmother, holds him as an ingredient.

Even the bird's timing is pure brother, right before a wedding, what most people would regard as a joyful event. This is typical for my family, who treat happiness with suspicion. That very morning, I congratulated myself on completing the transition into normalcy without their destruction.

The bird and I both know he has been the silent member of our conversation all along.

If it helps, she says, *you won't find him.*

"I won't find him," I agree. "Because I'm not going to look."

Do you know where he is?

"I assume in the city somewhere, hiding in a theater."

How long has it been since you've seen him?

"Seven years?"

The last time I saw Tom was at his own wedding, where he lay bloody on a gurney, asking me to hold his hand. *It's just that I'm so deeply unhappy*, he says, in memory. I remember the taste of vanilla and his anemic, furtive fiancée, Sara Something.

You're not going to find him, but it's important that you try, she says. *You'll do it.*

"I won't."

Her narrow eyes narrow further, narrow more. *Where are we? What's this murky room with only a couch? It's like we're in a stew.*

"It's called an antechamber. A room before a room."

A room before a room, she says in that way she has, that cuts through our tense and familiar squalls. *And what is your job?* The non sequitur means to stall until she can figure out another way to get what she wants.

"I work with people who have traumatic brain injury. Normally they've been hurt in car accidents or on the job. I tell their life stories in court. Like my client Danny. He drove a big-rig dessert truck and was injured while filling it with gas."

I guess somebody doesn't like Sara Lee. The room's grip releases. She performs inventory of what on her hurts. *Pain is different now*, she concludes. *It's more like sound in another part of the house. But I still hate my ass. Asses like ours never leave, even in the afterlife.*

"You don't have an ass," I remind her. "You're a bird."

A bird today. Myself again tomorrow. We could disagree for eternity but there's no one I'd rather sit with. I spread jam onto a scone and hold it out for her. *Where does it come from—beat a dead horse?*

"Probably from people who like horses."

Or hate them. Her beak cannot find purchase on the pastry. *The afterlife is truly cruel. Being a bird is exhausting. I'm obsessed with cleaning these.* She runs her beak through her tail feathers.

I ask what she's learned about humans by being dead and she says, *They ask for signs a lot. They're always looking for proof like, If you exist, rattle the mailboxes. But you never asked for a sign.* She quiets. *You never reached out. Why?*

"I asked once and it didn't happen."

And you never asked again. It's like a song.

"A song," I say, and she says, *A sad one.*

"What is it like?" I say. "To age and die?"

A sigh flutters through her corduroy belly. *Aging is easy, like falling down a hill. No choice involved. It's reconciling yourself to loss that's hard. I was eighty-five when I died. But I felt nineteen. I used to forget how old I was. I'd talk to you for long enough I'd think I was you. Then I'd look in the mirror and think, ack, who's that old woman?* A burst of shivering compels her from one cushion to another. *Had I been anything other than a sheltered fool I wouldn't have worried at all. I had the slut gene. I should have used it more. It's in the family. You walk across the room, people pay attention. It's not because we're beautiful. We're gnarled things who look like we've been pulled from the earth. Root vegetables: potatoes or turnips. Half of us miserable, the other half deluded. You've seen pictures of your cousins. However, we are possessed of the self. All arrows point toward us. A blessing and a curse. Not your mother, she was born complaining. Believe me, I was there. No fun at all. That will always be her fault because I made life nice for her. She married a man who couldn't summon up enough juice to break a glass and lives her life doing cross-stitch, the only thing she's ever liked. She's rich enough now that she can afford to be good at only one thing. You kids don't like your mother and I can't blame you. But it's a mistake to assume she doesn't feel pain.*

The bird warbles, a mournful sound. As a girl, I liked to press her supple lavender cigarette case against my cheek. *She was a real bummer, your mother.*

"She still is," I say.

How'd we get talking about her? Let's get back to the main event. Me. And how I didn't use my body enough. Those of us with able bodies have a responsibility to use them as much as we can. Given another chance, you wouldn't believe how I'd use it. Threesomes. Foursomes. More-somes. Smoking is a joy of life. Good lord, why did I ever give it up? My teachers called me disruptive. I should have disrupted more. In 1975 the most stunning man I'd seen up close approached me at a convenience store and asked if I'd go to his hotel room to make love. I'm holding a soup can and a bag of oranges and am not a woman men cross streets for. I say no, because I was married. What a waste of a waistline. What a disappointment life is most of the time. Divinity opened itself up to me in aisle four and I said, nah, I'll just be taking these oranges. If it came around again, boy, I'd meet it. And I'd smoke like a house on fire. Disrupt! Disrupt! What fucking else are we here for?

She is a rueful bird endowed with death's clarity, but she is misremembering her life. It is my mother no one crosses streets for. My grandmother caused car accidents.

In short, the bird concludes. *With regard to aging. Compared to the alternative, I recommend it. But you! Thin eyebrows. Pressed hair. You've been trimming yourself like a hedge. Do you realize you're still alive? Would you recognize yourself if you met you on the street?* She flits from cushion to cushion as in life she'd shift from foot to foot. *So! You're getting married! Et cetera!* Blood-colored sparks flare from her tufted neck and fade. She burns and spits. *You're thinking there's no harm to it. There's no philosophical right or wrong about making bad decisions. You're correct. Lie, be a shitty friend. No one's keeping score. Be as much of a dick as you like. Shitheads get as far as the nice. You can wait for justice.* She pauses as a hack of shivering overtakes her. *It's not coming. Where it lands is your ability to hear music. You can't tame yourself over and over and expect your self-worth to keep its shape.*

Her rebukes hammer a tender place only she can access. "Stop," I say.

Morning sun emerges through the curtains. Outside, an Inn worker shakes a trash bag into a breeze. I can't imagine searching for my tornado brother during a regular week, let alone the one in which I marry.

"I've made my choices, Granny. And I'm grateful you're here," I say. "Have you ever missed someone so much that the missing gains form, becomes an extra thing welded to you, like a cumbersome limb you must carry?"

She tacks. *Dramatic.*

"I can't do what you're asking."

Do it, she says, and I say, "I'm sorry. Anything else."

She rises from her perch into an eruption of flapping feathers. The commotion grows violent. A loud, clutching whistle. The outline of the beak and feathers wobbles and expands.

The bird disappears.

Replacing it is my grandmother-shaped grandmother, frowning with a human mouth, legs crossed at the ankles. Her skin is dewy and hair neat, as if instead of being interred for ten years she's been at the salon having her hair reaffirmed metal gray. Death has not been a good diet. She is still barrel-shaped due to a lifetime of keeping a chocolate drawer in the refrigerator where others store cold cuts. However, her affectation is gentler, out of focus, as if whatever light is illuminating her is losing wattage. Like the bird, her eyes are lined in blue. Zaftig from sweets. Except for the sour smell, it's her, undeniably.

I understand the reasoning of whatever force sent her as a flying thing because when I see the unmistakable thickness of her thighs, the ashiness of her November calves, her herness overwhelms the strand tethering me to calm. Now that she is present

I miss her intensely. My throat constricts and issues a sorrowful coughing spasm.

Emotionless, she waits for me to settle.

There is no anything else, she says. *If you can't respect a dead woman's wishes you're a disgrace. Mark my words. If you defy me, shit's going to get fucked up. After it gets fucked up, it's gonna stay fucked up. And after you can no longer bear it, it's gonna get more fucked up. The things you do to make it less fucked up are going to fuck it up even more.*

She dims. I hold out my hand. She doesn't accept but clucks (still bird) in disappointment. Affection, like crying, is a bother and a waste of time. *I don't want you to suffer. Find your brother.* Her body vanishes, her neck fades. *Dress short or long?*

"Long," I croak.

I would have gone short. You have my gams. I always got compliments.

Her hairline rewinds over her scalp. The painting behind her comes in and out of focus. A pastoral scene of a carriage in a field of corn.

"Don't leave," I say.

She's gone. I experience her death a second time. The birdless room carries on with the climbing sun, Band-Aid-colored carpet, carriage and the corn, seeming so undisturbed even I wouldn't believe there's been a specter sitting in it. The woman brightening the world has left it again, without ceremony or sound. Not one feather remains. Even the stench is gone.

Rose doesn't answer her phone. I consult my face in the mirror to see if it has registered any change but see only the flat cheeks of a woman late for an appointment. I dress. My suitcase is still packed because the honeymoon suite is currently being occupied by another bride and groom. The Inn overbooked and regrets the error in the form of a free bottle of champagne and occasional check-in phone calls that please no one.

In the main room, I find my wedding dress, strewn across the tablelette, covered in bird dirt. That troublemaker grandmother bird has disseminated her business evenly from its sweetheart neckline to its hem. The piles of gauze are thick with shit, the destruction so complete I marvel. When did she do it? I was with her every moment. No dry cleaner would be able to repair it in time.

I take the elevator but when I reach the lobby, the doors do not open. The lit panel near the ceiling confirms: lobby. I check the panel, the door again. Stuck. I call the front desk.

"This has been happening since the renovation," the concierge says. "Still a few kinks. The new generator doesn't have the same lid. A bird flew into it. James said it was fixed, but then."

James, I think. I think, *Joyce, Stewart, Baldwin.* "A bird?"

"Like it had a death wish," she says. "The weirdest thing."

The elevator's walls are composed of mirrors. I watch myself wait. The box makes a triumphant ding! The doors fly open as if the issue had been only mine.

In the lobby, the concierge notices my grief-stricken pallor and apologizes. "Getting stuck in an elevator can be so scary."

"It's not that," I say. "My grandmother died."

"I'm so sorry." She is immediately sorrowful. "When?"

"Ten years ago." I cling to the banister for support. The landing knob comes off in my grip. I hand it to her.

She slides it into her cardigan pocket. "We're falling apart," she says. There are still good people living on the Earth. She bears witness to my tears, rests her hand near mine on the banister I'm positive in a month will be garlanded in tinsel because it's a perfect banister for that. I remember dancing with my brother to the Cars in our socks and one of my clients who was hit by a truck while walking and now doesn't understand the idea of a face.

The concierge's kindness emboldens me to confess. "And she shit on my wedding dress."

"Yes." She whispers, like it's a password: "Family."

Danny lives in a three-bedroom standalone in Coney Island. Heavy weather and the ocean's nearness give the house a terrarium feel. When I arrive for our final interview, he is red-eyed from sleeplessness but for once in pleasant spirits. He scuttles ashtrays from the coffee table to make room for my glass of water. Sits on the couch while I sit on the recliner. After a few clarifying questions, I will be finished with him forever. I want to leave and think about birds.

Danny worked as a big-rig driver for a company that produces the cheap dessert products popular in six-year-olds' lunch boxes. He was refilling at a truck stop when the apparatus holding the hose cracked. Industrial hoses weigh a ton. This one fell onto his head and pinned him on the pavement, shattering his pelvis against the plinth.

In the diorama I've built of his life, a wife with box-blond hair, a young son in a karate uniform, and a dog named R2-D2 stand in a kitchen covered in Post-it notes. Like many of my clients, Danny uses these strips of paper as surrogates for the parts of his brain clear-cut by that hose. Over the course of several months, I've interviewed his family, doctors, fellow truckers, grade school teachers. I've plotted their anecdotes on a careful timeline I will present in court, chronologically to elicit more sympathy and a bigger settlement. I will ask the jury to imagine young Danny posed against lockers, popping an orange against his biceps. Studying for his trucker exams at night. I map pain to show what medical charts can't—how he can no longer coach his son's karate class, volunteer at church, pet his dog.

Danny flicks an ashless cigarette and bounces in place on the couch, occasionally checking the door leading to the kitchen. Crates are stacked along the wall, magazines piled on the floor. I smell fish and char. "You baking?"

He frowns. "Nah."

I'm undermining him if I check, but the smell of burning thickens. We enter the kitchen, where hundreds, maybe thousands of reminders blink in the occasional ocean breeze. I never escape the sensation I'm being surveilled, except instead of a penetrating gaze they are commands, observations. DON'T FORGET RICE. PETER IS THE COUSIN WHO STEALS. AN HOUR IS SIXTY MINUTES. CLOVER HATES LILIES. TAKE SHOWER. Some are so old the paper has become cloth soft.

Danny plucks one from the wall. SALMON IN THE OVEN. "Damn."

He opens the oven door, releasing smoke. "Oven mitt," I warn when he is about to barehand the rack.

He pulls out a blackened piece of fish, throws it onto an unkind pile of eggy dishes in the sink. "Trying to be healthy. Hopeless."

I write: GO EASY ON YOURSELF with a smiley face. I show him before attaching it to the wall where the previous note had been.

Clouds silver with rain over his cluttered yard. Atmospheric condensation aggravates already aggravated bodies. My clients normally bail on rainy days but Danny never cancels.

His pelvis healed, but it's the invisible injuries that make him feel submerged. His friends, flannelled, soft-spoken men, showed up regularly throughout his hospital stay, helped his wife, Clover, fix a makeshift bedroom on the first floor. They were confused when Danny still couldn't work a few months after returning home. It didn't matter how many times I explained that brain injury is unseen, they wanted to see it. Injuries, like god, require faith. Clover resents the burden placed on her salary. She takes out-of-town jobs that pay more. Whenever Danny mentions her work, he uses his fingers to place quotes around the word.

I don't share anything about my personal life with my clients. Friendship creates an unhelpful bond.

Danny fills a pitcher with water as R2-D2 gallops into the room to nuzzle my thigh. He is a two-year-old unexercised and panicky Labrador who looks as if he will at any moment speak. Everything in him wants to run. R2-D2 hunts scraps on the floor underneath Danny, who holds the pitcher brimming with water. I worry about his grip, but he wants to tell a story like an intact man about a fair he went to where a man balanced on top of a Ferris wheel. A tremor grows in his forearm.

I say, "Why don't you let me hold that?"

"Are you listening? I'm talking to you." He sways as if regaining his balance. The pitcher slips silently out of his grip, barely missing the dog as it shatters against the floor. R2-D2 yelps, scrabbles out of the room.

I collect the chunks of glass. "Was I holding that?" he says.

"Don't move," I say.

He says he won't but forgets.

"Don't."

He roots in place. I've never raised my voice to him.

"Did you drop the pitcher?" he says, when I am transferring the large chunks to the trash can.

"Yes." I guide him over the mess and into the family room. I motion for him to sit and hand him the remote. I wipe the kitchen floor and take the garbage to the outside patio where several other bags are stacked. The dog jogs beside me, sniffs a tree trunk.

On the train, I scoured online listings for wedding dresses, and e-mailed the sellers. *Shotgun wedding*, I joked. One of the brides has written back including her phone number. She signs the e-mail, *Yours, Ada.* My aggravation with Danny transfers to this woman's salutation. How dare she be so trusting, personal. How dare my grandmother arrive at the last minute and make demands.

In the bathroom, I dial the number. I've cataloged every item in the sparse medicine cabinet: the knife on the shelf, the jars of baby oil crusted with disuse, Clover's curlers like bright smacks against the earthen walls.

"Hello," I whisper. "I'm the bride who e-mailed about the dress."

"Hello," she whispers. "It's nice to sort of meet you."

"I'm at work," I apologize. "I have to be quiet."

"Why am I whispering?" I hear a giggle. She readjusts to normal volume. "Would tonight be okay to pick it up?"

"Absolutely," I say, and she says, "I live on Fourth Street."

"Which one?" I say. "East or West?"

"Northeast," she says. "By the park."

"I didn't know there was a Northeast."

"You'll have to try it on while you're here," she says, as if this thought has just occurred to her. "You'll want to make sure it fits."

"I'd be grateful."

"Absolutely," she says. Our word for the conversation.

"Is Northeast Fourth Street where the historic brownstones are?"

She says, "By the park."

Footsteps behind me. Danny stands in the doorway, glaring. "I don't have all day."

Ada and I make final agreements and hang up. I follow Danny into the family room, apologizing without mentioning the reason for the call. He is upset, perhaps because he does have all day. Like most of my clients, his marriage is splintering. It's challenging to be around someone in pain. People worry it will get on them. When I was hired, my boss, an injury attorney whose collar is never completely folded over the back of his tie, assigned me a book called *The Reptilian Brain*. The cover is a drawing of a reptile in the act of contemplation. The head is transparent, its brain waves represented in blue squiggles that emanate out of the parameters of the jacket and into the world, this suggests, into the reader.

A reptile's biggest fears are isolation and immobility. Most of my clients deal with both. "Think about the reptile," my boss reminds me. "How the reptile in you responds to the reptile in them." I am encouraged to phrase my reports in reptilian terms.

A reptile wants anything there is to want—the sun, your best ideas, the center of the center of the eclair, everything. It wants to flip itself inside out and emerge a new and shiny reptile encrusted in star matter. It wants to sit on a blanket with its friends, dominating everyone. It wants to control storms. Our waking reality is their dream state, and vice versa.

Who's driving? my boss writes in the margins of my reports. *The reptile or the human?* I think it is the only book he has ever read.

Danny's synapses are unreliable and finicky. Even if they convey the whole message, they can't be trusted to keep conveying it. You are holding this pitcher. Continue to hold this pitcher.

"How many Percocet did you take today?"

"Two when I woke up, and two before you came." He checks his pill case. "Maybe more."

R2-D2 scratches at the back door. For the dog the only thing worse than being with Danny is being without him. Danny wants to watch an episode of an old sitcom but I want to finish the interview so I can leave.

"We only have a few questions we missed from last time, then done. Sound good?"

He mutes the television. "Do you think that sounds good?"

"Please remember I'm here to help you, and that your answers will not be shared with anyone except your attorney."

"And the whole courtroom," he says.

"Not without your permission. Number five. Are you able to achieve erection whenever you want, occasionally, or not at all?"

He flips through silent channels. "Not at all."

"That means never." I read the questions quickly, in an even tone. "Have you achieved erection at all since the accident?"

"Once or twice."

"That would count as occasionally."

He punishes me for the enthusiasm. "Check me out," he says. "Brad Pitt coming through."

I write: *occasionally*. "When you achieved erection, how long did it last?"

"A minute or two," he says. "Not long enough for Clover to go for hers."

"Are you able to ejaculate whenever you want, occasionally, or not at all?"

He shifts in his seat, stalls. "If I can't get an erection, how could I ejaculate?"

"Sometimes in sleep, you're able to . . . without really . . . also, it is possible to ejaculate while having a flaccid penis."

"You'll have to teach me that trick. What's occasionally again?"

"Anywhere from one time on," I say.

He hears my impatience, pouts. "Write down occasionally."

Danny used to be quick to joke, according to his friends, but the accident triggered another man's temper. He yells at Clover, the kid, the dog. He doesn't even walk the same, Clover told me. This personality change is why certain lawyers present brain injury cases as fatalities. The client's first life has ended.

"Are you able to go to the bathroom without assistance from anything or anyone?"

He waits for a truck commercial to finish before answering. My phone vibrates in my pocket with messages, e-mails. "I'm able to piss but not the other thing," he says.

"You're able to urinate," I say. "All the time, occasionally—"

"All the time." He lifts the waistband of his jeans to show me a diaper.

"How do you relieve yourself of fecal matter?"

He points to a stack of medical supplies in the corner. "I use gloves to remove what I need. Six or seven times a day. I don't know when I have to go, that sensation or whatever is gone. I keep checking." He slumps into himself on the chair. He's crying, shoulders shaking, holding the remote like a sword.

I want to tell him that tears are a bother and a waste of time. "This is normal for someone with your injury," I say. "Most of my clients can't achieve erections at all."

"I lied." He pats his crotch. "There's nobody fucking home. I sit here and diddle my life away as my wife screws everyone in New York."

"I'm sure that's not true." I check my phone. The florist, Sam.

"You're weird today. Distracted, jumpy. Phone calls. Why are you so anxious to leave? Hey." He launches out of the chair with surprising speed and stands over me.

The self I put away during these interviews returns as I slide my phone and book inside my purse. I am alone in a house with an unstable man who, even injured, can physically overpower me. I must leave without upsetting him further. "That's good information, Danny. We can stop."

"That's it?" He shakes his arms over me, as if trying to rid a tree of fruit.

Excited by his owner's motion, R2-D2 leaps up and down against Danny's leg, barking.

I stand, my bag already looped over my shoulder. "I won't bother you anymore." As I walk to the door every atom in the room takes on the wrung-out nature of incident.

As Danny's adrenaline wanes, his pain returns. He sits on a pile of magazines on the coffee table. "Sometimes I feel like I'm watching my family from far away. Like they're on a stage and I'm in the nosebleeds. There's even a little me, a little Danny. I want to join them but my limbs don't work. I want to say to the little me, stop fucking everything up. My voice gets stuck. After a while, I think, well, why don't they find me? They're too far away. They may not even be my family. I may be using all this energy to signal to the wrong people. Do you know what I mean?"

"It's disassociation." I pause in the doorway. "A lot of my clients have it. You're not alone." I want to think about my grandmother. I want to buy a dress and get married so something new can happen.

"You got somewhere to be?" His volume reaches its highest and most pained register. His loneliness is tangible, it could leave with me and ride in the passenger seat of my car. "It's no fun sitting with the crippled guy?"

His pleading eyes match my own peeled insides. Against my better instinct, I decide to be honest. "The truth is. I'm getting married. You're my last appointment for the week."

"Married." His eyes brighten. "That's a happy thing." He pulls a faded wooden box from a shelf. He lifts the lid, revealing a gun. I open the screen door and step outside.

"Wait," he says. "That's just what's sitting on it. What a shitty thing to do," he apologizes. He holds the gun as if it is a delicate bird. Placing it aside, he removes a paper from the box. "A poem," he says. "A good one."

"Why do you keep a poem in a box with a gun?" I say.

"I like it." He studies me. "Maybe I'm dumb. Will you read it?"

"I'm no good at poetry, Danny."

"Okay, but keep it," he says. "I hope he's a good . . . man?"

"Yes." I am surprised by this consideration. "A human man."

"I didn't know whether you liked men or women," he says. "You're like . . ." He makes a muscle, gives a bodybuilder's pose.

As I've been many times during our interviews, I am insulted and flattered. "He's a . . ." But like when explaining the Internet to a bird, my mind empties. ". . . very hard worker."

"You got a bridal party?"

Another reason you don't tell them anything. The digging. "No," I lie.

"Brothers? I can't imagine you with sisters."

"Brother, singular," I say. "Older."

"No one understands you like your siblings."

"I'm sure that's true with many siblings but not with us. We don't talk. He's . . ."

"An asshole?"

My laughter surprises both of us. "A playwright," I say. "Who likes to use other people's lives in his plays. And, last I saw him, addicted to heroin."

Danny's eyes sober. "That's serious stuff. It breaks my heart to think of kids getting hooked. They don't have the tools to get out from under it."

On television, a child dressed as Darth Vader attempts to move a dog with his mind.

"I used to be great at weddings." He raises his arms to hold an invisible partner. "Most men don't get how to partner. Please stay," he says. "I don't have anyone to talk to."

"I'm sorry."

Danny writes: DON'T FORGET TO GET MARRIED on a Post-it and hands it to me. He returns to his recliner. R2-D2 lies next to him, placing his head on Danny's knee. "Bye, pup," I say. Then, to Danny, "It actually is a lot of fun, hanging out with the crippled guy."

His eyes remain on the television as he flips through muted channels. "See ya."

I hurry down the street until the chased sensation dissipates. I stop at a DON'T WALK and listen to my messages. The florist reminds me that we have an appointment. Her certainty calms me, along with a message from Rose, who says she will join me after the movie. I am an ordinary woman getting ordinary married to an ordinary man. This thought fails to soothe.

A woman pausing next to me wears a coat over a red sarong. The light turns green and we cross together, reach the adjacent sidewalk in step. Our strides match though I'm younger and wearing sneakers. How is she so fast? We move down the street in such sync we may as well be lovers. I won't slow my pace because I want to get away. I won't move faster for fear of appearing aggressive. I hedge, debate myself.

I pump my arms subtly so she does not notice the effort. It is important this woman thinks I am winning effortlessly. My legs are strong from running. My pelvis is uncracked. My original heart beats solid in its cage. I have time to kill and the ability to see a movie in the city. Should I acknowledge the situation? A well-timed chuckle can engender camaraderie, even in strangers, but when I dare to check her face it is blank. She engages in no interior debate, unaware that she is doing the walking equivalent of doppelgänging me on the street. She is effortless.

I fill with unaccountable anger. Am I invisible? I should never have empathized. Fuck this woman's ease and what it reveals in me.

She stops unexpectedly. Without thinking, I halt, too. She is younger than I'd have guessed because she wears the coat of a much older woman.

"You're trying so hard." Her eyes are pity-filled.

"I—" I say, but have no idea how to complete the sentence, which she seems to know because she turns and proceeds down the street with enviable agility.

The movie is called *Beginners* and stars Ewan McGregor, a man who could easily be mistaken for another man. Perhaps this is why he is famous.

Ewan faces the slow, ecstatic dying of his father, played by Christopher Plummer, who comes out as gay, then spends the rest of the film enjoying a predeath Rumspringa, cavorting with a hunky boyfriend decades younger. Ewan meets a girl with laryngitis who has a nose I want to cover with my mouth. She is dressed like Charlie Chaplin and they end up on a gauzy predawn Los Angeles street. He offers her a ride but she says nah. They rollerskate down the hallway of her hotel. His smitten talking dog continues to ask when they will be married. Christopher Plummer is dying. Los Angeles waits by the phone for itself to call.

The theater's stilted, matter-of-fact air makes me capable of clear thought. Ewan McGregor's feckless, loose kindness reminds me of my brother, though in this moment everything does.

I remember Tom's wedding to Sara Something, when I was twenty-nine and he was thirty-two. He overdosed, survived. His tuxedo shirt slit down the middle by the EMTs, the pulsing of his blood over his chest. I wasn't nice about it. It came at the end of years of unanswered messages, sudden criticisms, distracted tones. I left him at the hospital, ate vanilla wafers in my parked car. After that we didn't speak.

Ewan McGregor finds himself, when on the precipice of connection, lacking. He does what he thinks is his best. It doesn't work. He does his actual best and the movie ends.

Descending the escalator I see Rose standing in her winter coat underneath the marquee. Pale sun blurs the buildings and lights up her pretty bun. I will tell her my grandmother visited me as a bird and she will understand the complexities of impending marriage. She will help me navigate this emotional terrain because we've spent our whole friendship dissecting the merits of everything from marriage to ice cream sandwiches. Case-by-case basis, both. A simple and moving thought, a friend. I am already calmed by the fact of her waiting.

The lobby's clock reads one fifteen as I push through the doors to the bright outside and say, "Rose." I love saying her name. When I say "Rose," and she turns, it means she's mine. I say her name and she makes a tinny *oh* sound as a frown creases her forehead. It cannot be disappointment because we have history longer than the entire world. I take her into my arms. Our hug lasts longer than she seems to think it will.

I point to her wallet. "Where's your bag?"

"At the office," she says. "Too much to carry."

"Not very safe in this town of crazies."

She shrugs me off. "Thanks, Mom."

Rose and I stood at seventh-grade gym mirrors in our sports bras debating whether we were ready to graduate to real ones. In high school we clipped boutonnieres to our dates' lapels, took photos on the carpeted steps of her mother's apartment. We learned to pull cigarette smoke into the part of the throat where important things go. We researched blow jobs and knew not to get so distracted by the shaft that we ignored the balls. We never, ever ignored the balls. We detailed our first sexual experiences to each other in reverent missives as we shed the veil of our baby fat. We were sacred, horny angels massaging the balls. We claimed to adore the taste of semen. We swore we were going to be famous simply for being ourselves, humble with the air of mystery of a jewelry-ad woman from our magazines, who checks her watch only to decide, fa-la, time doesn't matter! Acclaimed for our dance moves, synchronized with outfits that didn't match-match but winked at each other. Her mother remarried in high school and her family moved to the suburbs. My father had been dead since childhood, so I borrowed her stepfather, a heavily belted man who overused the phrase, *Okeydokey, smoky*. My mother couldn't afford any of the colleges that accepted me, but Rose didn't bring up the disparity in our situations. She never joined the others who mocked my skin color. We penned monologues to each other about our separate colleges, fascinated by who we were on the verge of becoming on our new campuses—hers leafy and liberal and mine in Queens, where I still lived in my mother's house. Rose never mentioned my taciturn mother. I fretted in the waiting room of her abortion. When I spent a year in the hospital, she learned that ice chips allay anxiety. After we passed the age of fame she was still a celebrity to me, but after my injury, she retracted. She answered her phone less frequently and rarely accepted any of my offers to get together. Immediately after accepting the groom's proposal I asked her to be my maid of honor. What I love most about being engaged are the opportunities to see her.

We poke at chicken salads in a Union Square deli. Rose can

take long lunch breaks because she practically runs her medical journal. A large fern walks by with a serious-looking woman.

Finally, I am capable of telling her about the bird visit. I explain that the closer the wedding gets, the smaller I feel, as if the world's rooms are being taken away one by one leaving me alone in my junior one-bedroom apartment.

"I went downstairs to borrow toothpaste from the concierge—"

"You forgot toothpaste?" Her tendency is to leap to the story's point, though she always guesses wrong.

"Really, I wanted to talk to the concierge. I was putting off writing place cards, come to think of it."

"What are you even doing in the city? Aren't you supposed to be taking it easy in Long Island?"

"It's *on* Long Island, not *in*."

She frowns. "That doesn't make sense."

"They're oddly serious about it," I say. "I'm here because I have this florist appointment." This isn't entirely true. I had been shaky at the Inn and wanted to see her. Her expression, as if I am a pile of laundry she hopes will be put away, makes this sentiment foolish. I keep it to myself. "I don't think I want to get married."

She asks, Did he cheat on me, is he abusing me physically? Emotionally? Did I find something out about his finances? When I answer no, she shakes sugar into her coffee, confused. These are the only acceptable reasons for not wanting to be married. "Does this have anything to do with your injury?" I like the way she says it, face-first. Most people mention it as if wincing under a low ceiling.

"It has nothing to do with my injury," I say. "This insane thing happened—"

"I'm finished." She pushes her chair away from the table.

"I'm finished, too," I say. "Shall we walk to the florist?"

"I think I can manage that . . ." She glances at her phone, which glows with messages. ". . . but it has to be quick."

We cross into the park. It's early November but still warm. People who work in bordering offices scurry across the square holding their wallets.

"If I were to ever get married," she says, "I like the idea of a destination wedding."

At any opportunity—a penny hurled into a fountain, 11:11, driving by a graveyard—she's wished to be married. Our ideas of the institution differ; hers involves immutable contentment, me a roll of the dice. I don't understand why we are talking about her hypothetical wedding when mine is actual. ". . . an island," she says, "or maybe New England."

"New England is beautiful in the summer." My voice sounds pinched and alien, as if it's coming not from me but from the man nearby ridding his sleeve of crumbs.

"I like warm climates," she says. "Strapless dresses. One of Nancy's former coworkers went to a wedding in Barbados I think a few months ago. The pictures were incredible."

My wedding is failing against one that a former coworker of Nancy's attended in what Rose thinks was Barbados. A man on a bench forks noodles out of a plastic box. A girl walks by, clutching her wallet.

Rose says, "I wish I looked like that in jeans."

"You look great in jeans," I say, then, "Nancy is the one who undermined you in that meeting."

I expect a reward for remembering this friend fact, the meeting that angered her for days, but receive none. Are we going to get back to me? Rose speaks in a professional tone. "Nancy's been a pal, actually. Last week she put me up for a series about psoriasis that would mean a lot of money. She can't help the fact that she's had to be tougher to get where she is. Nice girls don't get the corner office." She says the last sentence as if referencing a movie we saw together. Disgust ticks her eyebrow.

My heart thuds then is still for so long I yearn for the thudding.

"I was always so fierce in saying I didn't think discrimination existed, that everyone was being judged fairly. I'd pitied other women who had to use things like misogyny to cheer themselves up about not being as talented."

"Talented." My neck stiffens, shot through with sudden cold. I focus on her hand holding the phone, the black squirrel pausing in its work.

"But recently I've seen it—the thing that happens when a less deserving man gets ahead for no reason. It started when Matt was given the article about suicide in Japan to edit when I had been the one who brought the story in. He'd only been there a few weeks. 'Where's Kyoto?' he said, when we first talked about it."

"He didn't know where Kyoto was," I say. "I'm sorry," I say. "I have to stop. I'm not feeling well."

I sit on a nearby bench. After studying it, she sits next to me.

"Could we talk about what I mentioned earlier?" I say.

"Your doubts?" She circles the word.

I silence my ringing phone. "My anxiety is high," I say. "A lot of factors and questions. I'm wondering if I should get in touch with my brother."

"Tom? Now?"

Put your hand on your heart and see what's happening there, I tell my brain. My brain delivers the message. My hand moves to my chest. Underneath the chilly skin my heart flutters.

"Is that a smart thing to do before the wedding?" Rose says. "He has such a destructive effect."

"Maybe not Tom, but Adrian." Adrian is my brother's manager and best friend.

"Adrian?"

Rose has become a bird whose particular call is to exclaim the name of people she doesn't like. Press down on your chest, I tell my brain, the pressure will jump-start your heart. Instead, my heart skitters.

"When was the last time you saw your brother? His wedding? I still can't get my mind around that catastrophe." Rose turns as if identifying the source of a bad smell. "What's going on with you? You look dead."

There've been several times in our friendship when Rose and I reached what I feared was its conclusion, when an important update to our subscription to each other had lapsed, and we either had to renew or face the tenuousness of our connection. Several years before, I had dated a married man whose cruelty put me in bed for months. In the conversations Rose and I had after the breakup, I'd often been accused of misremembering details and being dramatic. If I tell her the truth, she'll say that's what I'm doing now, exaggerating my nerves into the shape of a bird, so instead I arrange my features into a lively smile I hope pleases her.

"It's nothing." My voice comes from the direction of the carousel where ponies with hard hooves and ears shift by. They don't even go up and down anymore, I think. Just forward. Be positive, I tell my brain. "You would be great at writing about psoriasis." I hear the dandruff of trash on the curb of the Forever 21 building. If I can find my ChapStick and apply it, the darkness won't come. I locate the tube in my bag and swipe at my mouth. I steal a few cleansing breaths.

"I haven't told you the specifics," she says.

"You'd be great at anything." If I can swallow a sip of water, the darkness won't come. "Do you have water?" I say reasonably.

"You know?" She is annoyed by my sporadic attention. "I should get back to the office."

My vision collapses, pinwheels. I can see only the woman near us overturning a lunch bag into a trash can. My heart tries to leap farther than my rib cage.

Calmly explain to her that you are having a heart attack.

"I'm having a heart attack," I say.

"One of your spells. Even the thought of your brother can bring one on. This is what I mean." She flattens the back of her hand against my forehead. "It's your imagination."

The buildings that hover over the trees wobble, they will morph into malevolent shapes and descend on us faster than my ability to explain. I can only close my eyes and wait, as she guides my body to a supine position on the bench where pigeons shit. No living thing has a problem living today. The joggers in their bright trunks. A man chuckles into a phone. The crumbs hopping in the breeze, even. Even the crumbs. Meanwhile, my heart and mind are collapsing. Rose traces the length of my arm.

"Maybe loosen your coat," she says.

"I need it to be the way it is."

"Breathe then. Pay as much attention to what is leaving your body as what is entering."

Focus, brain. The sound I make when I inhale is metal falling into other metal, and it relents for only a moment before my chest sucks whatever it can back in. My breath serrates.

"In and out." Rose is penitent. I realize how much she wanted to leave, that my time had been allotted. "You're having a panic attack. Breathe." Rose says I'm fine to a stranger asking, "Is she okay?"

"Who was that?" It's coming, my brain says. Only you can see it.

"No one," Rose says. "It's in your head. Imagine your breath as a fishing line cast out slowly. Let it go as far as it wants. I knew you should have taken time off."

"I have to work." I don't say, I'm not like you who can afford anything she wants, but we both hear the unspoken irritant through the magic of best friends.

"Right," she says. "Your clients need you. In and out."

"Try loosening her coat," says another stranger. I'm being observed, as if I am a plastic can drummer or a woman painted gold who only moves one millimeter a minute.

Racked with guilt for delaying her, for making what sounds like a handful of strangers worry, for occupying a bench during a busy weekday, I want to make her laugh. "I am a woman painted in gold who only moves one millimeter a minute," I say.

"Sure." She sounds distant, as if looking in a different direction.

My heart steadies. My brain calls on the other parts of my body.

"She's fine," Rose says. "She's about to get up." Then to me, "You're causing quite a scene. But now you're telling jokes. Maybe you're okay?" She pulls me to a seated position. I open my eyes. Two or three people stand nearby, gaping. One of them takes a picture. "Nice," he tells himself. He walks off, fiddling with filters and platforms.

I'm exhausted and sweating but have regained control of my heartbeat. I assume Rose will wait until I trust my body again. "I need to tell you about a bird."

"Ugh," she says. "Birds." Her gaze is fixed on the stoplight where she will cross to her office. Her entire body points away.

"I'm fine," I lie. "Go."

"If you're sure." She dusts my cheek with a kiss. A waft of vanilla bean before she moves away. "I'll check up on you later today."

"Be safe," I say. "You always cross on the red. If you do that and get hit—"

"—I won't be able to sue," she finishes. "I know. Don't worry about me." She hits the word *me* in a way that will annoy me for months.

My phone rings. The florist informs me that I am half an hour late and asks if I know how many days there are until my wedding. I only have to say yes to her final design, but she'd prefer me to be there.

"We're not coming," I say. "Ever."

"Ever?"

Rose allows a group of tourists to pass, then tees up at a curb. The stoplight is red. I watch her wait.

"I mean today," I say. "We're not coming ever today."

"There are five days until your wedding," the florist says. "Long Island is far away. The longer you wait, the less chance you'll have to veto the design. Already this is an unusually late final appointment."

"I know time is passing," I say. "I know Long Island is far away."

"Tomorrow?" she says.

"Tomorrow," I agree.

We hang up. The light is still red. Everything is taking an unusually long time. Through weddings and showers and stoplights. Poor Rose waits.

Around this time, maybe even this day, a man Rose met through the groom will call. Maybe they talk about a leftover remark from a gathering, a kernel of conversation he's been nursing like the kitten I found in the backyard and fed with droppers and it yowled so much I feared it was some other wild thing. He asks her out. They arrange to meet at a neighborhood bistro. She'll tell me that part. Nancy and Rose will travel to Houston on business. Rose will tell Nancy about the neon phone she had as a girl and Nancy will tell her about the woman who stalked her in college, the reason she can't wear shorts. Nancy's trust in Rose will bloom and she'll put Rose in charge of Texas distributors. It will be travel and a few unclarified family obligations that she'll use as excuses the first few times she ignores my messages. Weeks will go by and I will glow for her job and this new boy. If she's happy I'm happy. Is she happy? I'll call again. I'll e-mail. I'll catch fractions of conversations at parties, mentions of her like glimpses in a store window. Other friends will hear from her, but I'll blame unfortunate timing. I won't ask anyone how she is, because our friendship has never needed outside sources. She and her new boyfriend will spend a long weekend at a mountain house. I'll see photos online. Only then will I acknowledge a disturbance in our wire. The logical part of me will advise staying calm, and I will, even when I see more photos of her and the boy and new people who wear the statement necklaces we hate. Our mutual friends will act like shuddering horses when I ask if anyone's heard from her. Antonia will return from a trip to Vietnam where she spent the entire time arguing with her girlfriend. We'll stay on the phone for hours. *The most painful thing was spending a month watching her fall out of love with me.* Rose will roll her wheeled suitcase through the airport. Stand in line, wait for coffee. Airports are scrubbed from particulars, you can forget a friend or a family while, from a list of tantalizing options, selecting a sandwich. One day on the phone my mother will say, "She ghosted you," but I'll protest: You don't have friends, Mother, so you don't know this is merely one of those times in a friendship when you're the kind of out of touch that dissipates with one visit. Further, she can't be a ghost because ghosts are present, avian, ghosts have unfinished business and Rose will seem finished with me. The subtraction of her will leave me feeling like the remainder. My entrance into rooms will trigger an easily detectable sealing of conversation. What Rose and I are to each other is the combination to my high school locker, indelible in the muscle memory of my hands. I'll remember that even though she never joined the girls who made fun of my skin color, she never intervened. That in high school she yearned for a boyfriend so much she'd ditch anyone. My irreversible idea of our friendship will flicker. The times I rescued her will occur to me on nights I will not sleep or eat or read. And then. Antonia, long over the breakup in Vietnam, will call and say, "Have you heard?" Never anything more wonderful or terrible than *Have you heard?* Something in me will fall from floor to floor to floor to floor to floor to floor to floor to floor to floor to floor to floor to floor to floor to floor to floor to floor to floor. The boy proposed, Rose and he will marry soon. I want you to hear from someone who cares about you, Antonia will say. Everyone is thrilled. Everyone loves the Rose she is with him. Everyone is invited, almost. I'll list friendship infractions. I'll want credit for every canceled dinner, for the affection I failed to receive. Two times around to the right, eight, one full time to the left, thirty-four, one time around to the right, eleven. I thought interest had been accruing. Like Skee-Ball machine tickets several arms long we traded in for a spider ring. The quarters don't buy you the spider but the time spent trying for it. Eight. Thirty-four. Eleven.

Of course, in the Grandmother part of me, I'll have known all along about Rose, maybe since she left me in Union Square with breathing exercises I could learn from the Internet. She was an endlessly ringing phone.

After I brought that matted, violent, bleeding thing in from the rain and nursed it back to health I swore it was a subway rat, or another terrifying thing I didn't have the word for but that you don't bring into your house.

This moment during which I sit on the bench and Rose crosses the park is the last time I'll be with her in the undisturbed house of our friendship that shelters our old posters, the sound of our living and undivorced parents puttering downstairs, our rides together on country roads we think we've named.

The stoplight is still red. I watch my best friend wait. On this afternoon in Union Square when we are still subscribed to each other. Which is why I breathe like a good girl in a way I hope will make her proud and ignore the fact that she didn't tell me to stay safe. I'm forever be safe-ing those who don't care whether I walk into traffic. Rose scrolls through what appears to be several messages on her phone. Maybe one is from him, the new man who will marry her on a gleaming hill far away from this city. I'll see one photo and close my computer. The light turns green. Rose moves with city purpose toward a side street. The ambition of her gait. The sagging hem of her skirt. My best friend. How can people pass her without realizing how singular she is? The way she holds her wallet in front of her like in the woods you would a lantern. One reliable thing in life is that people carry their wallets when they won't be gone long from the office. Their heavy pocketbooks left slung on the backs of their chairs. Rose didn't want to stay. I watch her turn the corner, so vivid when she's made up her mind. A falling anvil couldn't delay her and I am delayed by everything. The noise of the city returns and crowds me. I'm thinking how grateful I am for her as I remind myself to breathe in and out and in and out at lunch hour on an otherwise normal day in Union Square.

That evening I take the train to meet the woman who is selling her wedding dress.

A trumpeter plays in the subway car as we glide through the tunnels. I lean against the window in numbing, post-panic exhaustion. Between songs, the trumpeter adjusts her instrument and the car is silent. Other people board without realizing music has been played moments before, or perhaps the molecules are arranged differently than if there had been no music, so anyone who enters senses it, like they've walked into a memory.

What I first liked about the groom was that he didn't have to be drunk to dance. He'd pump his elbows like he was winding himself up. This is surprisingly winning. I liked his carefully arranged apartment, a stadium spice rack. His family are academics, framed certificates on the wall. I'm grateful to be marrying into a simpler enterprise. My family: a complex system of dark islands seen from land.

It occurs to me as we roar into the tunnel that connects Manhattan to Brooklyn that in less than a week I will be called wife.

My wrists feel hollow and I'm relieved when my stop arrives. The trumpeter and I exit at Fort Hamilton Parkway where she practices scales on the platform. On the staircase an overly coated woman halts in between steps to catch up with herself or wait for pain to pass, people grumbling by. What's easy for others is difficult for her. I walk behind, using my thoughts to help her until she reaches ground level and we part.

My phone rings, a number I don't recognize. When I answer, no one responds. "Danny?" I say.

"Hey," he says. "It's Danny." He pretends to be startled, as if I have called him. "I couldn't remember. Are you coming Thursday or Friday?"

"I'm not coming again, Danny."

"That's right," he says. "We're done."

"Lucky you," I say. "No more invasive questions."

I hear commotion behind him, a second of bar noise. "You say my name a lot. It's always, Danny this and Danny that."

"I guess I have something to work on." Travelers push through the metallic turnstiles one floor above the trains that arrive and depart dispassionately. I'm late but his voice prompts me to stop. "What's on your mind? Wanna talk?"

He laughs, a derisive sound. "Talk," he says. "Nah."

I ask if he's sure and he says, sure, he's sure.

"You take care, okay, Danny?" I say. "There I go again."

"Yeah. Okay." He has trouble hanging up. I hear more bar noise, fumbling, a muted curse, a dull click.

I find a dim street lined with photocopies of a silt-colored brownstone. One house looks into a mirror and sees its reflection. House and house and house. No one sits on any of the identical stoops. No one peers out the windows. In the distance, two blond women sit on a stoop. No, I realize as I get closer, two sister golden retrievers with large, emotive mouths. I contemplate asking them where I am but then their attention shifts to a woman bustling past, wrapped in a scarf, throwing up a vague scent of lilacs.

"Excuse me," I say. "Can you tell me where I am?"

She lifts her eyes skyward as if I've asked about the moon. "Brooklyn?"

The blinking curiosity, stubborn chin, and laugh lines remind me of someone. Her hand flutters to secure an errant scarf end and I know. It's as plain as the downward-curving nose on her face. I have run across myself on this street in Brooklyn.

"I'm looking for Fourth Street." I show her the address and she says, "That's my house!"

"Are you the woman selling her wedding dress?"

"Yes," she says, having fun.

"Are you seeing this?" I say. She retreats as if to avoid a swing. "That you look like me?"

"The resemblance is uncanny," she says. "I'm Ada." She holds out her hand to shake. "It's around the corner."

"Right," I say. "We spoke on the phone."

"Yes," she says. "You're getting married in a few days." Her mannerisms are what people have told me about myself. The absentminded way of dragging her fingers over her forehead. The pointed, blinking concentration.

"Nothing like the last minute," I say.

"If you wait until the last minute, it only takes a minute to do." Her horsey, off-putting laugh is what I've always feared about mine.

"It's been a strange day," I say.

"I'm sorry." She gestures in the direction of her house. "Come with me. We're clearly going to the same place."

We walk with an even pace, each with a tendency to glance

at each other midstride the way a swimmer breathes between strokes. We climb the stubby steps of her building, indistinguishable from every other on the block. She removes a single key from her pocket and opens the door.

"I'm making dinner for my husband, who will be home soon."

I recognize this thin safeguarding as a tactic I've used in the city. Her apartment contains an L-shaped family room and kitchen. Urgent wainscoting. A hallway runs alongside the main room, and through a farther door I see sweaters folded on a bed. The distressed, mismatched furniture of the content. Photo booth pictures hover over a small desk—Ada kissy-faced, Ada shocked, Ada pretending to sleep.

A cat sits in the middle of the room, expecting us.

"W!" Ada says, as if she assumed the animal would be out for the night. "This is my cat." W flexes its foot then from its seated position completes a leap onto a chair.

"Cats make a house a home." She unwraps her scarf, revealing the curly hair I'd have if I didn't iron mine. As she fills a kettle with water, the waves clarify and brighten her face. "Do you have a cat?"

"No," I say. "My mother was allergic."

"Do you live with your mother?"

"No. I live with my fiancé in Queens but this week I'm staying on Long Island."

She pulls out a tin of teas. "Would you like some—"

I say, "Would I," noting every contour of her face and body. *A dark, gnarled thing*, my grandmother would say. Ada doesn't wax her eyebrows or even trim them in any way I can detect. The courage this requires stuns me. Her dress bunches over her hips in an unflattering way. When she turns to arrange the kettle over the flame I see our enormous ass.

"Are you close with your mother?" I say.

She straightens. "My relationship with my mother is not terrible. She's . . ." Her eyes scan the wall as if it may contain the word.

"No fun," I say.

"Yes! Not abusive or overbearing. Friends of mine have close, wonderful relationships with their mothers. They know things about each other, like a secret crochet. My mother? She's fine."

The flame heating the kettle may as well be inside my chest. She has described the exact relationship I have with my mother. I say, "I'd like to ask you a question that I hate when people ask me."

"Indian," she says. "A town near Darjeeling. You?"

"Spanish Basque."

"The Pyrenees!"

We smile at each other.

She says, "Did your e-mail mention you already had a dress?"

"It was ruined," I say. "In a birding accident."

Her eyes register my answer's vagueness but she says, "Why do you hate that question?"

"Normally it means the person is trying to figure out how I'm different."

"But you're trying to figure out how we're similar," she says. "Anyway, I'm so used to it I don't mind anymore."

She yanks open a closet door and pulls out a dress. It looks exactly as described, if deflated, the way things present in person when you've first seen them in a photo. It is cocktail length, scallop hemmed, wide, wandering eyelet lace.

"Try it on?" She nods to a bathroom.

"Yes." I am here to try on a dress, I remind myself. Any Beckett play I've managed to wander into is odd weather that will pass.

I bring the dress to the bathroom and close the door. My job has taught me that private bathrooms contain essential information if you know how to look. A long mirror by the tub. One moderately priced shampoo. Simple, clean. No beauty items spill out of the drawers, in fact, I see none at all. The medicine cabinet contains a single comb and a book of matches from a bar called the Forest. It's as if the bathroom is for show.

I slip the dress over my head. Unsurprisingly, the length is perfect. Loose in the chest, to my chagrin. I can tell the gems that highlight the scalloping Ada described in the ad as otherworldly are fakes because they don't carve light like real stones do, stones that have received consideration from a knife or an ocean. Ada runs to silence the screaming kettle when I emerge from the bathroom.

"Twirl," she says. I lift the edges of the dress and sway. A derelict twirl, but she claps. She says she hopes she looked that beautiful in it and I assure her she did.

"We have nice gams," I say.

From a stack by the door, she finds a wedding photograph of herself and holds it up next to me. "Won't your groom go crazy for you in this?"

I cannot remember a time the groom has expressed pleasure or displeasure at anything I've worn.

The sound of a gentle knock on the door.

"Hon," a man calls. "I've forgotten my key. Could you let me in?"

Her face fills with upbeat expectancy. "There he is." She opens the door and kisses the man who's standing there. They peer at me with the bashful smugness of the newly married. I recognize him, pedal backward, and hit the kitchen table's mean side. The button-down's pressed collar, the sleeve of tulips clenched in his fist.

When we met he told me he'd overlook my light skin and winked like an antagonist in a novel. I had never had a relationship that was only for hotels. Lobbies, fresh towels, key cards. There was one hotel we particularly liked, whose rooms were shades of pink, like having sex in a peony. It was near a luxury supermarket that sold what I'd call beautiful foods. I'd fill my basket with fennel, ramps, fat-eared pastas, things I didn't have at home. I'd preen in the hour before meeting him, thinking that somewhere, every part of him headed toward me.

His wife performed what she termed "spontaneous" plays. Meant to be wild and unique, they always looked exactly the same. I knew them from the coffee shop. I remembered her arid face that never seemed to welcome. The woman who elbows me in the grocery line then turns, face peached with shame. I didn't see you there, you're so tiny!

He said Nigerians made the best lovers because they do it all the ways. Like most straight promiscuous men of that track, he believed himself to be a champion of women. This was important self-deception because it enabled him to cudgel unwanted affection with no accountability, and would be news to the women who, like me, had the sensation of being trapped in a revolving door. Sometimes clear air, sometimes stuffy interior, depending on where you were in the rotation. Chatty one day, dismissive the next.

I was not allowed to ask when, how, or what time. Never enough towels, doors with finicky relationships with their key cards. The craving hurt. He and I took jokes too far and conducted night-ruining arguments. I'd sulk on the hotel carpet, carpet another thing I did not have at home. I participated in my own subjugation as if watching myself by helicopter. A little me, silk-slipped on a bedside, waiting. Eating scraps. Not a peony. A garden-variety mistress. The husband's phrasing exact-unspecific, his tone grave honest. Duped, completely. Trapped and turning. His knife smell could halt my heart.

After I was injured, his texts and calls dwindled, until he was only a blinking name on a social media site he kept carefully out of date.

"Is this a joke?" I say.

He consults Ada for reference and I understand: I am merely another version of her. Her. This pulls an important fixture out of my kindness. "Hon?" he says. "Who's this?"

"She's here for the dress," Ada says. "I've asked her to join us for tea."

"The more the merrier." The words are tinned, false. He wants to be alone with her. I am an obstacle.

Ada tips hot water into three mugs. I have trouble hating her, though I do, because she makes his eyes shine as he watches her pour. Able to reconstitute a night's plan if it pleases her. For me, he remained out of reach, at some party whose details were spotty, or changed last minute, or I had apparently misunderstood. Suddenly the offbeat items displayed casually on the room's shelves are designed to bruise. A joke trophy, a model of an apple.

"It's an exact replica," Ada says. "He worked on it for months. The level of detail astounds me." She beams.

He worked on an apple for months? I peer at it. In its reflective skin, my narrowed eyes.

I sip my tea as an old desire to press my body against him grows and becomes the only emotion in the room. I decide to seduce him while wearing his wife's—my—wedding dress. I choose a seat on the couch next to him so Ada must take the chair.

"Do you live in Brooklyn?" the husband says.

Ada answers. "She lives in Queens but this week she's staying in Long Island."

"On," he says.

"On what?" She blinks.

"The correct way to say it is, on Long Island."

"Isn't it wonderful, how words work?" She smiles. "Has any-one seen any good movies?"

I tell them I have recently seen a movie called *Beginners*, about a man who has been lying to his spouse for several years. Only after his wife dies is he able to be his true self.

Ada asks if he's the actor who was recently on that television show, she cannot remember which? I lobby possible shows until we settle on one that both of us suspect is incorrect.

The husband balances the mug on his knee. "Sounds selfish. Lying to your wife for years."

My neck warms. "Anyone who'd think that hasn't spent thirty-nine years in a relationship they couldn't talk about."

"He was ashamed," Ada says. "He couldn't be free."

The husband says that hiding corrodes an important part of one's self. His hypocrisy makes me a fearless brat. I say, "None of it matters in the long run."

Ada mimics my furious face.

His spine straightens. "There is an objective moral code you cannot deny."

"For humans," I say. "Who also don't matter when you think about it." I fill my voice with the edge that implies he has not ex-amined this or anything very deeply. "That's the kind of thought that is good on paper but doesn't hold water in a practical sense."

"It holds plenty of water," he says. Whenever he was dismiss-ing my viewpoint, he'd sit like this, one leg propped over the other, at ease. Frat boy resting face. "Life is not a series of easily trackable moments that lead to a big decision. It is imperceptible shifts over time along a line."

Ada gazes from him to me. How can he, who views arguing as foreplay, marry a girl with nothing to say? I've turned on her. She may as well be a stranger. When she tries to speak I interrupt her. "Not for everyone. Your views are myopic."

His eyes lose their mirth. "It must be difficult thinking like you. The world's victim."

"What is happening?" Ada says. "We're having tea."

"Well, it makes me happy," I say. "Are you happy?"

"Happy," he says, as if testing the word. He worries it is a trick question, which of course it is.

"Happy," Ada says, feeding him a clue.

He couldn't be farther away from me and still be on the same piece of furniture. The couch is faded linen and like everything else in the apartment affects a relaxed glee.

He inhales deeply, but Ada speaks.

"I'm happy," she says. "This apartment is small but I have everything I need. Only yesterday I bought a trash can that fits underneath my desk." Realizing she is referencing things I don't know, she explains. "I'm a computer programmer and work from home. Before, every time I had to throw something out I'd have to walk all the way to the kitchen. I'd keep a collection of trash next to me until I had to go in there. Now, anytime I want to throw something out, I can. Instantly. It's luxurious. What a strange conversation to be having," she concludes.

Ada is the aggressively positive woman you pray your ex won't end up with.

We are interrupted by a knock on the door and look at one another, confused. In the doorway, a woman holds a set of keys in one fist and the hand of a little boy in the other. "Your car is blocking me," she says.

Ada collects her keys, apologizes to everyone, and follows them outside.

The husband and I are alone.

"I'm sorry if I was brusque," he says, carrying his mug to the sink. I move in to him and cover his mouth with mine. His body is leaner than the groom's and contains more kinetic energy I realize as he tenses in shock. With reflexive loyalty I notice he has the long limbs the groom has always wanted, as I take his hand and place it underneath the dress. He strains to escape my grasp. I palm his cock, then slide my hand inside his waistband. He is stronger than the groom. He shakes me.

"If I've made you think this is appropriate, it's not." He is calm.

I experience television miniseries logic. He pretends my advances are undesired but our attraction is so intoxicating I don't mind destroying Ada's night, their family room.

"I can't believe you don't want this, too," I say.

He relents. His mouth is warm and I remember how easy it was for him to get me off. Even the well-meaning groom's most earnest fingering can't make me come. He pushes me away. "I don't," he says.

"Hello?" Ada stands in the doorway. "What's going on?"

The husband tells her he did not participate, that he is as confused as she. I collect my clothes from the bathroom and shove them into my bag as I walk to the door.

"Who are you?" the husband says. "Why are you here?"

"Where's your wife?" I demand.

"I'm his wife," Ada says.

"You're not. His wife is a performance artist who writhes around onstage in a giant sock."

He exhibits no acknowledgment. I say to Ada, "You're a nervous breakdown. Some odd panic I'm having about my life. You're me," I say.

"I'm me," she insists.

"This is the narcissism of the millennial." The husband speaks as if narrating a zoo exhibit. "She came here because of an insecurity inside of her that demands an audience. There's a resemblance between you two, that's all." They stand against the counter in their one-bedroom where no one has to walk a long distance to dispose of garbage.

"Tell me about your spine," I say to Ada. "What is it shaped like?"

Surprised, she draws a letter in the air, a capital C.

"A lot of people have scoliosis," he says.

"What do your wrists and collarbones do when you're scared?" I say.

"They feel hollow," she admits. "I am me," she says, sounding uncertain.

"I am," I say. "I know because . . ."

My thoughts abandon me. I can't think of anything that would give me most claim to myself. My name? My driver's license? An amalgam of affectations associated with the customs of this particular time. A kit of proclivities. *Me* is possibly not a noun but a way of wearing one's hair. Just because I believe I am myself doesn't mean I am. Then I remember I have something that despite being given involuntarily shows up for me every day. I believe in it. It proves me.

"This," I say, hitching up the side of the dress.

Ada recoils but the husband stares straight on. "My god," he says. "What happened to you?"

"Do you have this?" My voice trembles.

"No," she says.

"You didn't? Get stabbed?"

"I don't have that." She lifts the side of her dress to show her seamless skin. "I'm sorry that you do."

On the gradient spectrum of *me*s, she is on the other side of pain. A peaceful, unharmed version. Less like me than people who aren't me at all, and this makes me fucked up and remorseful and desperate. I go at him. "You and I have already dated, though you're doing a good job of pretending."

"I've never met her," he says to Ada.

"You saw me every week for two years. We had sex all the ways, which turned out to mean the jackrabbit, like every other guy. You told me my skin was the color of everything you liked. Nicotine. Coffee. We went to Williamsburg, Virginia, together."

"He's never been to—"

"I've never been to Virginia," he says.

"You hated everything but the hot apple cider. You drank like a hundred gallons of it. It was old-timey and served in a wooden bowl. Apple." I reference the apple sculpture as if it has done the damage. "Cider."

"What apple?" they say in unison, pronouncing the word as if it is preposterous.

"Apple!" I insist. But on closer inspection I see I'm mistaken. The apple's form has changed. I cannot understand why I thought it was a fruit at all. What I took for its mesocarp are the sides of a room. I see a bed, microwave, sink, all a particular shade of crimson that lightens under my gaze until the structure and the minuscule pages inside it glow not red but pink. It's the room in our peony hotel. All my wild assumptions meet near the perfectly rendered phone book posing supine, miniature pages naked under the swinging lamp.

I experience the peace of a paranoid whose delusions have proved true. "We dated. Even though you were married. Until you left me when I got injured."

The room pitches as I walk to the door and, still wearing the dress, pull my boots on.

"Who are you?" He latches on to my arm. I am a bird trapped inside another person's life, sensing its mistake and trying to exit against relentless glass.

"I answered an ad. I have to buy a cheap wedding dress because my grandmother shit all over mine."

He moves aside. I open the door and step into the hallway.

"Wait!" Ada says. "Payment."

"Let her have it. We don't need anything from her." He gives the word *her* all he's got, drawing a boundary around them to imply my worthlessness. He would condescend like this when we dated. But like the apple I'm no longer positive this is the fruit I think it is. His snobbery was never that pronounced, was it? Did arrogance stiffen his shoulders that much? I am misremembering. His eyes didn't carry that particular sadness in their corners.

At its heart this evening is based on a transaction, goods for sale, and if I leave without paying I'm stealing. I search my bag for cash but my hands won't work. Bills flutter to the floor. I gather them and hold them out. Neither of them wants to approach me so I leave the cash on the table.

In the hallway I hear her say, "Be safe."

I descend the stairs and push through the building's front doors, ask a cab idling in the dark, are you free, anguish trampling my request. The driver throws her high beams on, moves past me to the corner, turns, and vanishes. Goodbye, other life.

I pull my sweater over the flimsy dress and walk down a narrow street, numbed in darkness. Garbage cans are stacked in unlikely formations. The buildings replicate on either side, blurring as they advance into farther dark. I'm shaking with cold and nerves, rejection, the fucked-upedness my grandmother promised.

In my phone I find a picture of us from that time. We pose outside a park wearing black jeans. I'd asked a passerby to take it, knowing even then I was stealing a moment of legitimacy. In private places we were greedy and proprietary, but in public, we had no right to each other. You can tell by his tentative hand, not gripping but placed beside my hip, as if guiding a daughter to shore. The uncertain, elated postures. I can't decide if the man in the photo blinking into that morning's sun is the same one who minutes before slammed the door and said, loud enough so I'd hear, "Don't say be safe to that woman." I avoid pre-injury photos. What's the point of being reacquainted with my former body? It's obvious we're happy. My smile so pale and winsome I appear floured.

How lucky anyone is to have a friend who has seen all their changes.

Fuck, I think. I have to call my brother.

I dial Adrian, Tom's manager, who produces his plays and insists on his outrageous riders. He answers quickly, sounding pleased.

"I'm getting married," I say.

"Am I," he says, "talking to a bride?"

"An almost bride. In five days."

I remember how unguarded he is, graciousness rushing the line. "It's too fast," he says. "I'm not ready. We're too young."

"You might be but I'm not. Thankfully, you're not aging."

"I am. You haven't seen me in years." I hear an almost imperceptible fleck of sadness.

"It's been a while. I'd like to hear how my brother is?" I say, as if the thought has just passed on a bus.

He pauses long enough for me to regret the call and the entire life leading up to it. "Thrilling. How about tomorrow night?" Concern—whether for me or Tom I don't know—underlines his words. He asks if I want to stop by the theater to see the play.

"No," I say. "Yes. I think so. I may as well get every uncomfortable thing done in one night."

"Good. There are many things to say but I've gone blank. I promise I'll think of them by tomorrow."

"Me too," I say.

"It's noisy where you are."

I consult the street. Still empty. The leafless trees are silent. "Don't tell him I'm coming."

He promises he won't then tells me the lead is having trouble understanding "the whole parakeet thing. She doesn't get why a young girl would be obsessed with them." He pauses, wanting me to explain. But I'm not an expert on anything, especially myself.

We hang up and I plan. I will ride the train to the Long Island Inn and take a bath. Tomorrow, I will see my estranged brother and hope the binding spell that grips me will unhate me by the evening.

Grandmother, I pray, release me.

A tremor beneath the sidewalk rattles the cans. The ground undulates, so soon after the phone call that I think Adrian must be involved. Metal planters clatter on a nearby stoop as if in an earthquake. But New York doesn't have earthquakes, I think, holding on to a railing. It must be the subway.

A hulking form made from a vaulting rod attached to smaller rods prows around the corner several blocks away. Its features emerge—a jib comes into view, then a boom, an announcement preceding the full measure. A ship! Glowing blue and real. The vessel takes up the asphalt but its borders are suggestions, quivering harmlessly through parked cars as it moves toward me. Its masts loom over the apartment buildings. Its sails wobble elegantly in some other world's breeze, illuminating the buildings it passes through. Branches of trees and stars glint through its portholes as if its cargo is the woods at night. I widen my stance as the full rush hits then moves through me like strong-willed water. I open my eyes to a pellucid world. The garbage cans shimmer in a conceptual form. The trees are ideas of trees. I hear traffic several streets away as the ship populates me. I immediately yearn for the shock after it passes—this must be love. I who never give much or chase anything give chase down the street. Its masts and banners unfurl yet cause no wake on the asphalt so I am its wake, yelling hey, and hey, and hey! The ship accelerates. Hull fades. I halt, afraid that in my pursuit I'll miss whatever's left. The ship ambles around the corner, sails rippling once more, portholes flash then die. The mainmasts shine over the rooftops on the opposite street before gliding into another world, leaving me hammering and devastated, alone again with the other discards on the sidewalk where good and bad people have piled their trash.

M^y mother is being played by an understudy.

Wicked flu or something screwy with shellfish, Adrian guesses, filling me in as he leads me through the theater's nothing spaces—a chain of empty hallways, a staircase, a room whose sole purpose appears to be hosting a fire extinguisher, until we arrive in the open air of backstage.

I sit on a stool where I can remain hidden but see the action. The first act is over. The stage resets. On the house side, audience members talk in clusters while the parakeets perform a skit. This intermission play is borrowed from Shakespeare, related loosely if at all to the rest of the story. One bird delivers a monologue about the technology age. A bit with a phone, a tussle for laughs.

Adrian stage-manages around the city's theaters, surfing the theatrical seasons, in addition to representing my brother. Any theater company wishing to produce one of Tom's plays, especially *Parakeet*, his most lauded, must sign lengthy riders specifying nonnegotiable terms. No word may be changed in the dialogue, no genders switched, no actors doubled. My brother won't allow the interpretation commonly practiced in the plays of Shakespeare, even though he grew up obsessed with him, insisting I call him "the bard." As a boy he'd deliver urgent monologues, pronouncing each anon, forsooth, good sir with the solemnity of a priest, the crotch of the thick tights he'd steal from me ballooned against his thigh like a tumor.

My brother refuses interviews and has sent Adrian in his stead so many times that people suspect Adrian is the actual author of the plays—a Marlowe-ian mistake that no doubt delights Tom. Our estrangement has always devastated Adrian though he respects it with polite deference, like excusing oneself around a pointed table that takes up the entire room.

After the skit, the parakeets vanish into the array of curtains that flank the stage. They pass me and move deeper into the flats, an impulse of feathers. Adrian points above our heads, where they reemerge on the catwalk. The trembling of the floor as the stage activates to a new setting could be my heart as I wait to be unmoored by whatever appears.

In the play my name is Luna and I am an only child. There are four Lunas in *Parakeet*: Luna at eight, Luna at fourteen, Luna at twenty-three, and Luna present day, the "narrator."

Lights up on coffee shop. Luna at twenty-three arrives for her shift. Her coworker tunes in to a rock station. The thrum of music being flipped past comes through the overhead speakers. An arguing couple enters.

The overall effect of this faux shop is dustier, meant to evoke gritty realism, I'd guess. Tom wouldn't have known certain details. The radio was tuned to Yuna's favorite cooking show. The couple was not arguing, but asking each other what flavor ice cream they wanted in that way some couples have that invites others in. Ironically, my brother has omitted the writer, who had spent the previous week grousing over an award that was given to a woman he considered undeserving. I'm grateful for the buffer these differences create that enables me to pretend I'm watching the worst day of someone else's life. Memory follows the logic of a dream or poem. Even as the half-accurate scene plays, I recall details obscured by time. Yuna planned to attempt macarons that weekend and promised to bring some in for us. I am the only person on earth who knows this.

Though I've never seen *Parakeet*, I've read every write-up. The dimensions of the set's dinner table, around which all plot points occur, is specified in contract pages the potential director must initial. As the scenes tick by, Luna collects more stuffed animals. When the animals enter in the last scene, they are to be ordered in a way that is also specified. The birds must be with the birds, the horses and zebras together. A director cannot substitute a dog for a fish.

Many articles speculate about Tom's retreat from public life. He's an organization helmed by committee, a criminal, a group of women. Much has been written about why he won't permit interpretation of *Parakeet*. That he believes in time-capsule art, that he is a misogynist maestro. They're all wrong. Baffled companies who want to produce this odd, violent heart of a play are not being held to the specifications of a playwright, but of a little girl.

We were hypersensitive, sickly kids, constantly made fun of in school. Every day my classmates reminded me I was different though there was little chance I'd forget. They'd mark my out-loud face as if doing me a favor: Your eyebrows are joined, they'd say. Your calves are not shaped the way mine are. Your mother looks like an Arab spy.

My mother demanded silence, but when we were together Tom and I were feral. One night, frustrated by our noise, she booted the door down and hurled handfuls of my stuffed animals into trash bags. Tom stood between her and them and widened his stance so he could not be moved. My mother backhanded him against the corner of a bureau.

The next morning, she dragged the bags to the curb. She seemed sheepish, no longer certain, but perhaps felt trapped by her passion the previous night. It was Saturday, when other families stenciled their walls or crocheted. I don't know what other families do. But I know our trash day was Tuesday because I watched the bags that held my animals get rained on for two and a half days, imagining them clinging to one another for warmth.

Three crows, two zebras, one whale, a handful of ladybugs, one unicorn with metallic wings, three horses—one pink, one green, one realistically colored—two butterflies, three bears including the one we got free with a wiper blade change, a dolphin from the aquarium class trip we lied to go to, convincing my mother she signed the permission slip while she dozed on the recliner after my brother made us a simple meal. Finally, four parakeets arranged up front, who were the young Luna's—my—favorites.

Place the walrus next to the puppy. The raccoon comes after the bear. The hush of human voices on the other side of the curtain, amplified and immediate. I had prepared for cruelty but not for this tender thought: Tom has returned my animals to me. They will never be out of order again.

The Man from the Coffee Shop enters and every conciliatory sentiment fades. Tom's gotten it wrong again. When the man entered in real life, no one noticed. There is no memory in a play. A play is always present tense. I am newly injured in real time.

After final curtain, Adrian and I climb the back steps to a shared dressing room. The Lunas are at the snack table, piling meat onto sturdy rolls. They say, Hey Luna, what's up there, Luna. When we enter, Luna at every age turns her eyes to me.

There is my grandmother in period clothes, tapping sand off her boot on a fake fireplace.

There is my mother's understudy, eating turkey on rye, half shucked from its wax paper. She offers me a sandwich, more mother than my real one.

Adrian introduces us and does not mention that without me none of them would be ten floors above Broadway, dragging baby oil–doused cotton balls over their eyelids. The director, a diminutive woman in massive glasses, asks to speak to Adrian. The cast exhibits the intimacy of weeks of constant contact, forgetting me to debate phone warranties, a sweater they should've bought. They have evolved into their roles. The director's monologue runs under the current yet I hear parts of it. She is still not getting— Present Day Luna, who refuses to— It's in the contract, even— Being stubborn, don't you think? And who, anyway? Talk to her.

As I wait for Adrian to finish I feel exposed and ratty and murderous toward my brother. I want him to show so I can punish him.

"I was hoping I'd meet the playwright," I tell my understudy mother.

She shakes her head. "Never comes to the shows. Notorious. We thought for opening night, at least. A real kook, I hear." Her eyes widen. "I'm sorry. I'm an understudy."

Adrian returns and announces that he and I will head to the diner to get a drink and wait for the others. He whispers to me that the donor dinner is wrapping up and we can expect to hear more soon.

On the empty stage, Present Day Luna stops us. She wears a silk kimono and smiles when we are introduced before proceeding with the errand she has with Adrian. The director wants to see her, she's going to say that thing again? Do you think it's right?

As Adrian listens, he checks me with an occasional glance. He is a bank where others invest their valuables. If he turns out to be trustworthy, which he almost always is, they increase their investment. Adrian assures Present Day Luna that what awaits her is nothing she can't handle. He and I escape to the cold street.

We secure a few tables at the diner. Glass of wine for me and scotch for him. We're alone. The years have lined his eyes and mouth as if he has deepened into himself.

"Are you as ready as you can be?" he says.

"Am I ready?" Parakeets arrive in street clothes, still wearing their wings. I slide to make room. They are named for the fairies from *A Midsummer Night's Dream*: Peaseblossom, Cobweb, Mustardseed, and Moth.

My grandmother arrives, having transformed into a sweet-faced girl with gray hair dye collected at her temples. Stagehands. A woman who identifies herself as Mary from the office. "I'm in charge of sales."

The director is not coming, someone says, because she and one of the Lunas are having a talk.

"Which Luna?" Moth says.

"Present Day," the girl says, like it's obvious.

Everyone says they know what that's about. Everyone knows that the father won't come because he's not the type to hang out. "He's probably upside down in a dungeon," Mary says. Everyone agrees. But then my father enters from the cold, bracing a parakeet head against his side like a fullback holds a football. What timing! The actors cheer. We had just counted you out yet here you are!

I am a secret here, but it's difficult for me to resist giving notes to my "grandmother." She was proud of her nose, I want to tell the girl. She was always touching it while talking.

My phone rings. It is the florist. Again, I've forgotten to stop in to see the mock-up. My thoughtlessness has baffled her polite. "When you originally said you'd pick it up instead of having it sent, I hope you'll recall, I expressed my opinion that I didn't think it was a good idea." The actors guffaw at someone's joke. I plug my ear with a forefinger.

"But you said," she continues, "'I'll be in the city, no bother at all.'"

"Please don't do my voice," I say. "That's mean."

"I'm sorry. I'm at a loss."

"Tomorrow," I say.

"What if you don't like it?"

"I'm sure it's fine. Look," I say. "I don't care."

"Queen Anne's lace."

I realize that she cares, it's her craft on the line. "Sounds beautiful." I hang up and apologize to the table of actors and crew.

"We're very lucky to have her here," Adrian says. "She's getting married on Saturday."

The actors applaud. Cobweb claps and hops in place.

Mary from sales asks where, how big, what time? As I answer, the parakeet sitting next to me shifts and huffs. Mary tells me that the best decision she ever made was choosing high cocktail tables for her wedding. Low ones are bullshit, she lists reasons. Normally the tendency of people like Mary from sales to give unsolicited lectures on menial subjects annoys me. Tonight, it seems quaint, benevolent.

I horrify her by saying I don't have preferences, I've allowed my mother-in-law to plan most of the reception.

The parakeet next to me sighs. "Do you hate weddings?" I ask her.

"Peaseblossom hates everything," Mary says.

Peaseblossom frowns. "I guess I don't get why everyone assumes a wedding is a good thing. There are a million reasons that get a woman into a wedding dress, not all good. Jealousy, aggression . . ."

"Merging of property," one of the actors offers.

"Property," she agrees. "Chances are you've been to a wedding where the groom is miserable. The bride, the parents."

"At my sister's wedding last year," a stagehand says. "She fell asleep during mass. The groom had to wake her up twice."

"That's anxiety," Peaseblossom says, pleased. "When a woman realizes she's lying down with the patriarchy."

"Does that make you happy?" Adrian says. Only I know him well enough to see the slip of his thoughts show. "Another woman's panic?" Adrian smiles, always managing the actors whether they're in a black box or a Times Square diner. "Open dialogue is important. Still, let's keep in mind there is someone at this table who is getting married soon."

The table's attention shifts to me. Peaseblossom is too young to know she should apologize, which I appreciate.

I don't mind the pseudo-progressive marriage talk, the bandying of hypotheticals by people who pretend for a living, though I hold a sisterly suspicion of performers. I've never liked how they handled my brother's gentle nature, doing violence to his texts, soldering them open with their coarse stage games.

"Have you ever been married, Adrian?" Cobweb says.

"Honey, I've been married hundreds of times." Adrian dons the parakeet head. He holds his ringing phone up to the papier-mâché ear. "Hello?" Everyone laughs. My grandmother helps him take the head off. He nods to me. "Yes, yes, we're all here. It's me, the Lunas, the birds . . ." I shake my head no to a question he asks with his eyes. ". . . and a few others. Come join you? A party?"

Everyone but me cheers.

Okay, I mouth.

We leave and walk through Times Square's after-hours daylight where dozens of families debate whether to stop at the mega chocolate store. Mary from sales wears the parakeet head. Every person at Forty-Seventh and Broadway sifts through their bag to find something and not one of them does. Leather satchels, wristlets, bags like corsages pinned to the wrist.

A man whispers into the vicinity of my neckline, "I am not secretive. You can see that I have a disability."

An elephant walks by. No, a man with a child on his shoulders. One hundred tired parents shoulder one hundred tired toddlers. A break-dancer spirals on a flat of cardboard. The actors pump their shoulders to her music. The beat drops out. The dancer halts, balances on one shoulder that supports the weight of her body. Palms pressed flat against the cardboard, her feet flexed and up-twirled to the haze of billboards and the starless sky. The dancer eyes us over one remarkable shoulder.

The beat returns.

She corkscrews off the ground, shuts off the boom box, jigs from person to person with an outstretched hat. The actors give her everything in their pockets. We say goodbye to the two Lunas who have curfews. One leaves with her mother, the other alone, both carrying parts of my childhood.

The party is in a fifth-floor walk-up above a major appliance retailer. No one appears to be the host. We pour drinks in the kitchen and take them into the main room, lit by the back of a neon sign, a refrigerator holding hands with a washing machine.

I sit on a hammock slung between two pillars, surrounded by parakeets. Every time the door opens I worry/hope it is my brother.

Adrian traces Cobweb's collarbone, making the young man giggle.

Mary slides coasters underneath everyone's drink.

Two men walk in. "Oh no," Cobweb says. "My boyfriend."

Adrian is still flirting. "Your what?"

"Boyfriend," the boyfriend says, crossing the room. He is not an actor, but someone who looks like he can build a bureau with his hands.

The boyfriend ignores Adrian and speaks to Cobweb. "Are you fucking kidding me, Marco? Jesus Christ, let's go. We have to go to your mother's tomorrow and I'm not disappointing her again. Get your shit, Marco. And don't forget your phone because I'm not coming back."

I can tell Adrian is impressed with the way this man and his friend navigate the room. We're all impressed. Adrian extends his hand to shake on an erotic, participatory idea, but this man will not engage. De-winged, Cobweb takes off his wig to reveal nonglamorous hair. He leaves with his boyfriend.

Adrian says, "That's one way to leave a party." A few weak titters. His phone rings. "Perfect timing." He disappears into the back and returns to inform us that there is another, better party uptown. To me, he whispers, "We're on."

"Now he's uptown?" I say, my resolve slipping. The change of locales, the citywide parade. "Is this what it's like every night?"

Adrian answers the question under the question. "Everyone is clean," he says. "No drugs. Please remember, you're not letting me tell anyone you're here."

"Let's go into the forest!" Mustardseed says.

We catch the train uptown. Adrian and I take the two-seater

and I lay my head on his shoulder. Birds flank us. Someone says, remember we have a performance tomorrow. Someone tells that person to hush.

Mustardseed insists, "Let's go into the forest. If it's locked we'll climb the gate. We'll pretend we're owls. We'll see the moon come up over the lake." How lonely extroverts make me feel. The train erupts out of the station and we hover aboveground for a few stops.

Adrian traces a circle on my shoulder. "Before we get there, you should know. The person you think of as your brother is not the same."

"I know recovery changes you. I work with a lot of addicts."

"There is a change," Adrian says. "But it's more than that."

We leave the train at Columbus Circle. The shops are closed, but one of the birds has stolen a bottle from the party. We pass it around and I regret my earlier thought about actors. Peaseblossom receives a message from Present Day Luna who has finished her director's meeting and is hurtling through the city in a cab. I hope she gets stuck in traffic and goes home, but then a cab halts at the curb and she leaps out, holding a white dog the size of a coffee cup.

"Well met," she says. "Tut tut."

"Tut tut," the company says.

Adrian zips the shivering dog into his coat. The park is snow-filled and quiet. Present Day Luna stands next to me, eclipsing me in height. I am far from the Long Island Inn. Shoving my hands into my coat pockets steadies this thought as we walk across a swath of lawn to a lake that is famous to all of us.

Someone says, "We should take off our clothes and go in."

Someone tells that person we'd die.

I follow Adrian into the brush. The thrum of whiskey, the

shape he makes against the banks of snow, and the nearness of my brother perform a trick. The snow is my brother. The dark path. With every step memory unwraps and I remember what it's like to be in a room with Tom when he's sober. His intense gaze, broken only occasionally by a laugh that changes his whole body. His patient heart. My own batters my rib cage. I want to tell him everything. I want to never see him again. I want hours of uninterrupted time to talk about our grandmother the bird.

The trees are ankled in fresh snow. The dog in Adrian's coat is asleep. The actors are finally silent, the only sound boots plunging through the crust. Our skin is illumined with crescent reflections moving over us, as if we are underwater or by a pool in all those movies about Los Angeles.

At the end of the field, a driveway winds up a hill to a mansion. Inside is a famous unicorn tapestry, a collection of wrought-iron tools, and, Adrian promises, the person I'm here to see. I stop halfway up the driveway so I can steady myself against his side to pull at my boot. He can look at me for as long as he likes without the uncomfortable prickle I experience when anyone else does because I know his secret, he doesn't care about any of these people. After this run he will move on, the way after a fun season you shutter a house.

Present Day Luna catches up to us.

"Did she tell you?" she asks Adrian. "About the note?"

Adrian nods, checks me for reaction. The dog in his coat gives me a sleepy wink.

"I think it's bullshit," she says. "I don't think she thinks that way at all." She peers at me, a question brightening her eyes. Don't talk to me, I pray. "Maybe I can ask you," she says.

"I don't know anything about acting," I say.

"I know who you are. We saw pictures. We all do, don't we?"

Luna asks Peaseblossom, who doesn't answer. "I'm sorry if this is pushy but I rarely get the opportunity to speak to the person I'm playing. The person whose life it actually is."

"It's maybe too late for character research," Adrian says.

I tell him it's fine even as the list of what I don't like about this woman grows, her insistence that she is respecting my privacy even as her ego pushes into it. She speaks with the wandering expansiveness of a woman who doesn't know we die.

Mustardseed points to the luminous, milky field. "The moon and snow are talking." But Luna won't be distracted. "Why is it important to tell this story?" she says. "No one can give me an answer. I'm supposed to represent Present Day, the perch of the story. But why now?"

"Beats me," I say.

She frowns. "And what's the deal with the parakeets? The play doesn't make it clear. I should know why she needs to replay these scenes from her life in this way at this time."

"It doesn't sound like a failure of the play, but of imagination." Her wounded expression pleases me. "Why are you entitled to know?"

"That's my phone," Adrian says, wresting it out of his pocket. "We're here," he says. "At the bottom of the driveway."

"Ask the person who wrote it, *why now*?" I say to Present Day Luna, gesturing to the house.

"I did. The answer was that I, Luna, blame myself for everything. The play is my unburdening." She glances downward as if doubting the ground. "You're right about entitlement. Every director I've ever had has gotten sick of my questions. Can I just say, though?"

I brace to hear something unforgivable.

"It's very clear in the text that the playwright loves you so, so much."

If she knew the damage this does to me she'd be the meanest woman in the world.

Adrian, on the phone, says, "I'll wave. Can you see me?"

"Look," Peaseblossom says. At the top of the hill a copse of old-fashioned lamps outside the mansion illuminates then goes black, ignites, goes black.

The company cheers, passing us.

"I have a surprise," Adrian says. "Your sister is here." The lamps go out. "Here, here. Not kidding at all. She saw the play and everything."

Luna lifts the tiny dog from Adrian's coat and joins the others. Adrian's smile turns from confused to concerned. He hangs up. "I'm sorry," he says. "It's not the right time."

"The right time for what?" The lamps turn on. A few of the actors reach the front door. "I can't go up?"

Adrian shakes his head. "I'll leave with you. We'll get a drink and talk."

"I don't want a drink." I shake him off, walk out of the park as he follows with Peaseblossom and Mustardseed.

Adrian insists on finding me a cab but first he must buy an orange juice at the deli. The birds with wrecked hair and lopsided wings scrutinize breakfast sandwiches from the counter menu.

If it helps, my grandmother said, *you won't find him.*

I buy a banana and rejoin Adrian and the parakeets on the street where they hold paper bags and gaze up at the trees.

"It's supposed to be sixty degrees tomorrow," Mustardseed says. "This snow won't last a day."

I admire Adrian's hips outlined in morning light, the elegant stance that makes him so desired. He says, "Don't let me live anywhere with no seasons again."

"For a moment," I tell him, "I mistook you for a woman."

He hits a pose, designed to beguile. "I get that a lot."

He hails me a cab and we say goodbye on the street. "Adrian," I say. "I don't know if I want to get married." As soon as I say it, it's true, and the wedding becomes a tangible, breakable thing. I understand that I am able to do things to it, like opt out.

"That doesn't surprise me," he says. "Look at you. Shocked I still know you. Whenever you're in fugue, you don't answer direct questions. You repeat what the person says." He pantomimes. "How do you feel about getting married? *I'm getting married.* Are you as ready as you can be? *Am I ready?*"

"Don't do my voice," I say. "That's mean."

He shrugs, smiles. "Life is mean?"

"Will you think less of me? The groom is decent and kind, has a good job, a promising future."

"Sounds awful."

"I have a dead-end job. Bad health insurance. It would take me years to pay this wedding off."

Above the rooftops, cranes add to the city, giving everyone more to work around. Mustardseed rustles in her coat, says *I'm cold* with the preserved sweetness of the early twenties. Adrian's breath puzzles out from under his scarf. He says, "You'll be a beautiful bride if you decide to be. Don't wait so long to call again. I'm capable of getting very angry."

"No, you're not."

"No, I'm not." He laughs. "I allow your family everything." He tightens his embrace around the birds. "You're so used to taking notes on other people. You know who that reminds me of?"

"He hasn't changed," I say. "He's still selfish Tom. Tell him I said so, Adrian. Tell him I said, Fuck his unburdening."

His gaze remains gentle. "You should probably remember that transition takes time."

One of the frustrating things about performers is that they're always exiting on a landing line. "Don't say something like that and leave, Adrian. Don't do it." He and the parakeets are already walking away. Every moment the snow diminishes. One thing is ending and another moves uptown limitlessly into the bargain the trees make with the morning. I want to join the thing that's limitless, I'm mixing up Adrian and my life, my love for a friend I never get to see, nights with him so rare that they're precious and they hurt.

THE BOYS WHO LOVE PRISCILLA

My brother's voice on my phone in the morning, *beseeching* me to meet him in the city. There is something I should know before being angry, which I am well within my rights to do, he admits in his message, because of the play, the years, what he calls the "Whitman's Sampler Assortment of Crimes" he's committed against me, referencing our grandmother's favorite chocolate without realizing the irony. I'm swayed by the well-placed intimate reference. Besought. His voice weapon and shield; higher-pitched than I remember, from what must be sorrow or lack of sleep. Then something I've never heard him say: I'm sorry. The audacity that repulsed me in the evening heals me in the morning and I show up to a public city atrium feeling manipulated, hopeful, confused, weak-willed, undercaffeinated, assuming the worst and hoping for it. Human.

Amid a bank of metal chairs and the sun, a misplaced-looking family consults a map. A couple shares a salad. A well-dressed woman folds a receipt into her purse. The family's mother says, "I understand." I see my brother, sitting in the farthest chair, partly obscured by a recycling receptacle, taking a bite from a sandwich. My legs tremble as I walk over, too nervous to call out. Age has receded his hairline and broadened his shoulders. He is almost unrecognizable.

"Hello," I say, standing over him.

He drags his fingers across the cellophane wrapper to clean them. "Hello."

"Tom?"

"Greg," he apologizes. "I think you're looking for someone else."

The other tables are brotherless. You won't find him, my grandmother said. I dial his number.

Yards away, the well-dressed woman answers her phone.

I watch her speak and hear my brother in the earpiece. "Are you here?" he says.

"Tom?"

The woman snaps her purse closed and stands, turns in my direction.

At an empty table I sit in a chair that hurts instantly as my brother walks toward me wearing a prim blouse tucked into black work pants: his movement edits the courtyard's sound; the lost family's reorganizations gone, the honking of morning trucks gone, to include only the tapping of heeled boots as I notice the obvious things first; the slimmer cheeks and neck but then as this figure comes closer I notice deeper, more familiar, stranger, the dark skin familiar, the flashing eyes familiar, the simple eyeliner and lip gloss new, my understanding has almost caught up by the time they reach the table—a woman, who moves like water being poured from a delicate vase.

The other chair squeaks as she sits. Her perfume finds me.

"You can hang up now," she says.

The family, oblivious to anyone having metamorphic moments nearby, asks one another how important it is to see the museum and the church in one day. Could they do one in the morning, before the airport? But the flight is so early. Well, whose fault is that?

"Do you work here?" I say.

"I keep an office on the tenth floor. I like being around businesspeople. No one bothers me. They're more polite than artists and don't ask questions."

"You've always liked your space," I say.

The mother of the tourist family stands above us. "Do you know how to get to City Market?" The woman I am sitting with gives careful, patient directions, as I study her for anything that remains of the person I used to know, the endless capacity with strangers even while wagging her heel underneath the table in anticipation of the mother leaving. The elegant hands, the voice that has always sounded like stacked bars of light. She concludes, "The city is a grid meant to baffle us all," to make the mother grin before she rejoins her family.

I experience the sensation of walking out into the sun after a long movie. My eyes won't adjust. "You're a woman," I say.

She says, "Yes."

"Do you have a new name?"

"Simone."

"Simone," I say. "Where did it come from?"

"I just liked it," she says, looking uncomfortable.

"Did you have a ceremony? It seems like the kind of thing that calls for a ceremony."

She nods. "A few of us gathered upstate. I have a house there now."

I swallow the pain this puts in my heart. "A house," I say. We avoid each other's eyes as we speak.

"Would you like me to tell you about it? It sits on acres of land. If you can believe it, I dig around in the earth. Me. I'm not going to be joining the garden club anytime soon but there have been carrots."

My laugh punctures the politeness. She relaxes.

"We made food and sat on the lawn. I was nervous, but a friend of mine had recently been through cancer and I thought, if she can be here . . . It was a filthy gorgeous day. I mean really it was greedy of us. Slight breeze. Air you could get drunk on. Even the grass was shining. The food was good, well, the food was okay. We did our best but the steak kebabs were dry. Another friend made a silly remark when she walked outside—a silly joke, but we were crying with laughter. Do you remember, a million years ago, when the old lady walked through the screen door? It was like that. Everyone in a good mood on the same day. I didn't want it to end. It felt like a sin when the sun set. But then the yard was filled with fireflies. I'd been in the city for so long I forgot about fireflies. I stood in the center of the lawn, everyone stood around me. I said, 'I'm Simone.' Everyone said, 'Hi, Simone.' That was it. We sat down and ate the crappy kebabs."

She pantomimes *eating kebab.* Her wrists are thin and mapped with veins, like mine. She holds this woman's grace and the person I used to know's ability to entertain with an offhanded gesture. She is simultaneous. Wholly present. Wholly past. Wholly grandmother. Wholly bird. I struggle to lace up my understanding.

At this hour the atrium contains only a few stray businesspeople, zagging to their particular doors. The couple at the table next to us gathers their things. Their kids run around the trash bin and the father yells, "Be careful."

Simone and I leave the sitting area and walk to a glass-walled restaurant. I am aware of her form, the rustling of materials next to me, as we move into the café, as we wait for the waiter to pull the table out from the wall, as Simone slides in and crosses her legs. After we order, she asks what I like about the groom and I tell her he doesn't have to be drunk to dance.

"How nice," she says, concern showing through her honeyed tone.

I tell her he's exact, a literalist. He taught me the right way to say *experiment*. "Ex-*spear*-i-ment, not, ex-*pear*-i-ment."

"Experiment," Simone says, not understanding.

"You're saying it the way I do," I say. "Say: Ex-per-iment."

"That's what I think I am saying. Ex-spear-iment."

We say the word back and forth until each of us forgets which way is correct. I tell her that he asked me to marry him on our fifth date.

We're not accustomed to having meals together, so one of us talks while the other steals bites from her plate: ahi salad in her case, soup and a panini half in mine. When it's my turn to speak I am more expansive than normal so she has time to eat. She replies and I take my own careful bites. We work together to avoid silence and in this painstaking way get through the details of our lives, half of our meals. Then the conversation launches, we each find an easy listener in the other, and I lose track of who is eating, speaking. I've never been to this restaurant whose fixtures, counters, and tables are built from glass, yet in it I realize everything can have a new name. Perhaps our relationship could, as well. We could be sisters who travel upstate, I think, then shelve the thought, as familial dread grows.

Omitting the visit from our grandmother, I tell Simone about the wedding, Rose, that the groom's family are academics. Each of them looks perpetually poised to ask a question after a great deal of thought. They're rich enough that each of them only has to be good at one thing.

"Must be a nice change from our family," she says.

"Do you know what they do when they're upset with one another?" I say. "I mean, furious, livid-upset?"

"What?"

I sip water, pause for effect. "Nothing. Not a fucking thing."

"How do people live like that?" she says. "Granny would burn the house down."

I study her face for an indication there is more behind the reference. "She would."

The conversation shifts. We perform irreverent jokes about unfunny, unjokable things, and unreel tiny parts of ourselves, testing, unreeling more, within fingertip's distance but not touching, almost like holding hands.

"I never felt altogether boy," she says. "I hated the places on me that weren't soft. It was more manageable as a kid because then we're all androgynous, but puberty came, and suddenly everyone's differences emerged. What my body produced felt incorrect. I prayed to be one of those guys who couldn't grow a beard, but the stubble grew almost as fast as I could shave. So much hair in our family."

"All those cuts," I say, and she says, "The cuts. I was jealous of how easy your body was. I wanted shoulders like yours. When the play did well, I was able to go to Europe. I started taking hormones, got work done, and liked it, so I got more. I finally felt like I was arriving. But everything has a price. I don't mean money. I didn't think I'd be able to see anyone from my old life again."

With *my old life* I am formered. "So you wrote a play about my life, won awards, took the money, and disappeared."

"I didn't think you'd forgive me. It's not your way. You're so good at holding grudges. It's one of your superpowers."

"You didn't give me a chance, though, did you? What do I do now? Do I mourn for my brother?"

"Maybe," she says. "He's not coming back."

A group of tourists walk by trailing the chintzy-clean smell of people who've scrubbed with products that can function as shampoo and toothpaste. What I perceive as her lack of loyalty to a person I love bothers me in a way that is impossible to articulate. "Did you mourn for him, for us?"

"I mourned through my whole childhood. I'm over it. I was relieved."

"Simone," I say, and she says, "Simone."

"You're used to the idea," I say. "But I'm only now hearing about it."

"Transition takes time."

"Adrian said that last night," I say. "He protected you. Do the actors know?"

"Legally, for the sake of my career, there are essentially two people: Simone, a person in the world, and Tom, the author of plays, most notably, *Parakeet*. Tom the playwright is elusive and mercurial. This arrangement might change in the future, but for now it works."

"We were coming to meet you last night," I say. "Your actors would have seen Simone."

"They've met me. You'd be amazed how easy it is for a middle-aged woman to slip in and out of a room unnoticed."

We finish our meals. Simone searches for the waiter.

"The actors were terrible," I say. "Especially Present Day Luna."

"You've always hated people who are similar to you."

Little-sister aggravation heats me. "You got a few details wrong," I say. "We didn't notice the man enter. And Yuna was a grad student. She was going into her second year."

Simone shifts in her seat. "I did the best with what I could remember."

"From my memory? I don't remember you asking, or even visiting the hospital. Not then or when Granny died. Engineering . . . ," I say, punishing, ". . . was what she was studying."

"It's fiction." Simone hands her plate to the waiter.

"It's not," I say. "It's my life. You got famous from it."

We split the check, walk to the street, and linger on the sidewalk. Anxiety I experienced whenever I left Tom has transferred to her. I want to hold everything on the street close to me.

"Can I see your house upstate?"

A dog passes, attached to a leash held by a stooped man. A waiter dashes from the restaurant to the street to hail a cab. "Let's go slow here," she says.

"Did you miss me?"

"I wish I could come to the wedding." She guesses my thoughts. "But for obvious reasons," she displays herself, "it's not the best idea."

On the corner, a man throws a baby into the air, catches him, throws again.

Simone starts a cigarette. "How old are you now, thirty-six? I guess that makes me almost forty."

"You look good," I say.

"You look like hell," she says. Too quickly.

"Sorry if I'm bothering you," I say.

"You're not bothering me," she says simply.

"I'm kidding. How could I be bothering you? I never see you."

"Right," she says, not understanding.

My anger blooms. "Is this how people apologize for using their sister's life in a play?"

"I hear that you're upset." She exhales smoke. "It was easier to talk about what I witnessed than what I went through. It was, just, easier."

"Your childhood was my childhood."

"It wasn't." She is managing me. "You clearly don't understand."

"You knew you were becoming a woman. Give me time."

"I didn't become a woman." Her eyes clouding over. Something slipping away. "I'm not sure why I thought this would work. What is the first thing you said?" She mimics my voice. "Where do my memories go?"

A pocket of quiet. Both of us breathing. We are arguing over who has it worse, which is at least what siblings do. I'm torn between wanting to yell and wanting to hold her, but anger makes me a snake. "Who fucking cares what my first thought was? You used my life to collect your awards. So brave."

"Realistic," she says. "I could get murdered for what I am." She loses her composure, which I count as victory. She opens the door of an arriving car.

"When did you call that?" I say.

A frowning man jogs past. A moment that means goodbye. She gets into the car. "I don't know why I thought this would work."

"You already said that," I say. I say, "If I told you Granny showed up a few days ago in the form of a bird, to tell me to find you, what would you say?"

"I'd say it sounds like her to show up late and ruin things." She shuts the door and the car moves down the street. Every stoplight turns green. I watch until it disperses among cabs and pedestrians. Numbed by pain the origin of which I don't understand, I descend the stairs to the subway where three boys perch on the hull of the subway bench, addressing another who wears a red scarf and searches the tracks for the train. The scarf is the color of Adrian's. This is the coincidence of cities.

"You got a girlfriend," one of the boys says. "Who is conveniently never around?"

"That's right," the boy with the red scarf says. "Her school's outside the city. In Long Island or some shit."

"In school," one boy says to another. "Okay," he says. "In school." He lifts one leg comically above the seat and puts it down.

"She's going to be a nurse."

More laughing.

I want to tell him to be silent because he's making it worse but instead I eat a banana over a trash can and replay Simone's remark, *You look like hell.* The last word a chop to the throat.

The lead boy reads texts from someone named Priscilla. A respectful pall grows over their faces. "It would be rad to see you," he reads. "Hashtag boardwalk, hashtag loser, dollar sign, dollar sign, two lipstick emojis." He holds up two fingers. "Two."

The other boys demand to see the phone he hides behind his back.

One advances to deliver a monologue: "Last week I was in the middle of the floor doing applejacks when Priscilla stopped to watch. She was with her friends who live up on Allegheny and I was like"—he sidles up on an invisible girl—"and she was like"—he does a girl batting her eyelashes, squirming with pleasure—"and her friends were like"—he shows his palms to his friends, slides away to give himself and the invisible girl privacy—"it was personal."

"No, you didn't," the boys say.

"How come I did, though?"

The boy in the red scarf slices through the air with a definitive no. "You all are suspicious. You don't believe shit."

"Look, look, look." The lead boy stands on the bench. "If you say you got a girlfriend who's never around, I'm gonna ask questions like, does she exist?"

The other boys help:

"Or, is she ugly?"

"Does she have a lazy eye? Or a hang jaw?"

"Hold up," says the boy with the red scarf. "What's a hang jaw?"

The lead boy lets his bottom jaw hang slack. Red Scarf shakes his head as his friends laugh. He hides a smile by checking for the train again.

"Is she an alien?" one of his friends says.

"Listen." The lead boy claps everyone to order: "Either your girl is ugly, has a hang jaw, or doesn't exist."

"Look, look, look," Red Scarf says. "She's not ugly or an alien. She's from Long Island."

They hit one another and repeat it. Red Scarf has to stand and take it as they collect tears with their fingertips. There's no reasoning with them through laughter this thick. "She's from Long Island," they say to one another.

A sign hangs over the platform. NOT FEELING LIKE YOURSELF? it reads. TELL A POLICE OFFICER.

I recognize a woman in a tweed coat as the trumpeter from the previous night. A dainty purse hangs from a chain on her shoulder. Without her trumpet she appears vulnerable, like seeing an acquaintance in their underwear. She catches me staring.

"No trumpet tonight," I say, by way of explanation.

She gives her purse a rattle. "Night off."

We smile at each other.

"I sense it, though," she says after a moment. "Is the weird thing. By my side, like I'm still carrying it." She gestures to the area around her left hip.

"Phantom limb," I say.

"Right."

Like a god the train enters the station, sanctifying every kid being given a hard time. I follow the boys on, certain Red Scarf is hoping the change of venue will cease the teasing. My ears brace for the peal of more laughter. None comes. Suddenly polite, the boys take seats near the door and I hold the pole. When the train lurches forward, a baby throws its doll. A father flutters across the car to catch it. So many parts of the doll are round that it builds momentum over the soiled floor. Strangers lean from their seats to help. It takes a few people but the doll is returned to the baby. The father is flustered and grateful. "Thank you," he keeps saying to everyone, even to people who didn't help, like me.

I will do a head-clearing shot of whiskey at the bar before bed. It will be a quiet day. I will eat breakfast in the pleasing room off the lobby. Maybe I'll run on the treadmill. Get a massage. Get trapped for hours in the Inn's moody elevator. Pick up my bouquet from the most ardent florist in the city. A dish of strawberries. Rolled newspaper in the hallway.

The train rumbles through the tunnel. Everyone is settled. Everyone is doing okay.

On Friday, the groom will arrive along with our families and we will eat shrimp at the rehearsal dinner. His normalcy will be a welcome relief from my bizarre, cracked relations. On Saturday I will be a woman in a dress stepping over a threshold into married life. A bride. I will finally leave my family behind.

I did what you asked, Granny. Release me.

Someone says: "She's from Long Island."

The boys done in by laughter again.

ENTER MOTHER

I wake the next morning from troubled dreams, leftover dinner marbled on the plate, glass of whiskey on the nightstand fringed with my lipstick, feeling less and more than, thighs spreading wider than usual over the sheets. The room is unchanged: bland knickknacks, half-unpacked suitcase spilling clothes on the carpet. Danny's Post-it stuck to the lampshade: DON'T FORGET TO GET MARRIED.

My legs require double effort to get out of bed but I reason this away, too much drinking. Punishment for disuse. I miss running for hours. It's over, I think. The running and all of it. The dismay of loss triples down and tears arrive. But this is nonsense. There's a fitness center on the Inn's fourth floor. I could go right now.

But you won't, a new, dark voice in my head sneers. Because you're useless.

I reach for the water, notice my hand on the glass, and drop it. It jackknifes against the carpet and throws liquid against my hairy calves. These nails are short like mine but unpainted, the knuckles raw and swollen. These fingers are mottled, not smooth and hairless. An unkind current courses through each finger as I try to make a fist. I experience a desire to withhold affection in order to force people to move closer.

I am the stranger I've woken up to after drinking. A shower will return me to myself, I think, running the hot.

My phone rings and the florist asks if I remember our appointment. "I do," I say, "I'm not someone who makes appointments and forgets about—"

In the mirror my mother stares back at me, terrified. The countenance I pin to all of my anxiety, that anticipates my failure. I make an uffing sound, a yank in my throat, as the phone slips from my hand. The florist hellos against the bath mat.

I hang up and spend a long time lying on the cold floor. I pace the hotel room asking myself where I am, what is happening to us. In the mirror I run a tissue under my sagging eyes, still wearing the topic of most of my therapy sessions.

Desperate Internet searches yield nothing helpful. *Transmogrify to mother.* "Feminist Nightmares," reads one article title. "Women at Odds." *Changing into your mother*, I try. "The 8 Stages of Realizing You Are Your Mother." "You Idolized Her, Now You're Turning into Her." You're proud of your Tupperware set, you ask the waiter to box up three bites of food, you don't recognize celebrities, you hate youth. Whose mother is this? Mine refuses to eat in front of other people, burns rice, prefers the company of young people to anyone.

You have her body parts, the article reads.

I can't imagine what is going on under my pajamas.

You sound like her, the article reads.

"Hello?" I ask myself. "Am I here?" It is my mother's deep, muscled chowl that launches a panic attack whenever I hear it on the phone, revving to ask a series of bruising questions. That stated while we were shopping for wedding dresses: "Better not halter," the horror, the horror. This throat is not mine but borrowed. I have taken up rent in my mother's body.

To complete this existential hemorrhage, I become aware of a third sentience inside me, blinking behind my mother and me—what I can only call "other mother." An amalgam perhaps of both of us, seen from a distance. Other mother is slower to judge. Perhaps she is from another timeline, the idea of myself as a future mother. She seems separate from my mother and me, contemplative, steady, sitting near but not with us.

I dress with my eyes shut. The legs of my jeans refuse to cover my new, horrifying calves. The dark voice, an inward sinking, trails me as I force this foreign body across the room. Why bother? it says. The fact that my mother is always pert and bristly makes less sense to me as I propel her into the bathroom, her body fighting me/itself. A loose dress fits.

Mother, what do you go through? You feel like trudging through mud.

I leave a message for Rose, then for the groom. I peer at her self in the mirror. I lift my arm and she lifts hers. My mother and I, finally in sync. Her coarse hair is cropped to the ears and the texture of thin wire. I comb it but it won't stay. She must use hot irons. My/her teeth are bonded. I run my tongue over the smooth porcelain, much better than my badly treated nubs. I've always been secretly proud of her complicated profile. I turn her chin in the mirror, admiring the way it cuts light. It is so visceral now that I possess it.

In addition to the obvious downsides of becoming one's mother, there is another, subtler loss. The buffering that comes from the slow passing of years turned out to be an essential kindness: adding plates one by one to the tray, instead of shouldering it all at once. Imperceptibly logging time on your waistline, cultivating theories into one impenetrable worldview, gradually developing eye and mouth lines while moving through trends, passions, pursuits that distract. Researching Thailand or new ways to make chicken, tiring of traveling and chicken, desiring evenings reading under a blanket, watching dusk grow in the garden you've researched and tended, incapable of thinking of a time when you won't want to watch a garden darken, until realizing that, too, was a phase, yearning to travel again, away from that chore of a garden, and all the work put into those plants only to have the rabbits outsmart you, the world is so cruel to small things trying to grow over time, under time, through it, years compiling throughout, and inches, replacing old fences, replacing those no longer new fences. Discovering new ways to love and shut love out, and all the while, the map on your face being clarified, but slowly, civilly.

Aging: revoked! Unmitigated change bears down on me. I collapse against the wall.

"I know you're angry," I say to Simone's voice mail. "But I'm having a very specific nervous breakdown and I need your help."

I throw a coat over her and leave the room. Knowing this elevator, I take the stairs, keeping my eyes trained on the floor as I scuttle over the lobby carpet, stopping to catch my breath every few steps. Mother, are you ill?

Sit, weakling, the dark voice says.

I obey and press my cheek against a couch cushion. The elevator doors ding and on the other side of the lobby I watch myself emerge from the elevator. Me, me. Is it supposed to be cold today? she asks the concierge. I wonder if my mother is inside, working my controls and marveling at the ease with which I move. But I sound unaffected, worried in a quotidian way but no more. Is this my voice? As a girl I trained myself into a sexy, breathy allure, but from a distance it sounds donned and embarrassing. High, curved, and citrus. No wonder everyone mocks it.

I watch my real self as I hide in my mother's body behind the lobby couch. Dear god, the ass. Inherited from my grandmother, that immortal spread. The dark voice says I should eat more healthfully, exercise like I mean it.

Another guest enters the lobby, overloaded with packages. A tiny parcel tumbles to the floor, where it lands by real me's sneaker, real me stoops to pick it up, returns it to the woman, and smiles in solidarity. Beauty! I am striking in an understated way. I watch myself walk through the lobby, the serious ass careens through the glass doors, and I'm gone.

I slink my mother's body into the breakfast room where croissants are stacked in pyramids. There are trays of sausage, grits, baskets filled with English muffins. Cereal vats with silver-tipped dispensers offer three varieties of milk. Speakers play piano music. The room has a honeymoon vibe but I am jumpy, cross. I cull a plate of eggs and bacon from the bottom of serving dishes.

"If you wait a moment," the server says, "we'll bring hot eggs."

"No thank you," I say. "I'm fine with the eggs I have."

However, when the new eggs come, their nutty scent compels me. I dish a heap onto my plate, second thought, dish another heap. Normally, I don't like them but now I am egg-obsessed, not even bothering to swallow before forking more into my mouth.

"Good." My stepfather takes the empty chair across from me. "I've caught you." He is tanned and graver close up. A woman at an adjacent table checks him with her eyes. "I understand it's hard to talk about," he says. "But I think it's important that we stay in dialogue. I never meant for it to happen. It was a one-time thing bred from loneliness. Heavy petting, really." He speaks in his usual infuriating way, as if lecturing recruits. "It's for the best. We can tell her after this whole thing is over."

Her. This whole thing. A waiter applies apples to a pyramid of fruit. "What whole thing?"

"You're going to play aloof?" He throws his napkin in disgust. "I'm going up to the gym. Clear my head. You could, too, you know. Take pride in your body."

"I could," I say.

"You won't, though, will you? Even though it's important to me. The smugness is on overload this week and it's only going to get worse when he arrives." He pronounces the word with an insider's inflection. *He.* "Say something," my stepfather says.

"I don't think the gym has a water cooler." I squeeze jelly out of a quivering packet. "You'll probably want to bring your own bottle."

He sucks in air, consults the serving dishes with obvious revulsion. "I can't talk to you when you're like this." He leaves.

It is my stepfather's voice she hears, internalized over time like a coastal shelf. My mother's body is almost immovable and she's wild for eggs. Her relationship with my fat-shaming stepfather is rotten and possibly over? What a classroom this nightmare is.

I slide into my coat. I must get her to the car, though every limb is flagged by upsetting gravity. It connects to the voice that says, *Don't*, which battles my nature that says, *Do.* You cannot, the dark one says. You can, my positivity counters. I argue with my mother. I berate ourselves. Just be a human, walking, I bargain with us. We walk outside, stopping to breathe. The lake rejects steam in the cold morning. I push the seat back and readjust the mirrors because I am a few inches taller than the day before.

I leave another message for Rose and for the groom.

I drive to the city and notice how the pedals are easier to maneuver with these longer legs.

"I'm a monster," I scream, when Simone calls. "I'm Mom."

She is calm. "Are you on ketamine?"

I tell her I woke up as the old lady, our stepfather is cheating, she's addicted to eggs.

"This is a twist on a joke, right? You find out I'm trans, you can't let me have this experience, you have to become an old lady?"

"I don't want to discuss the ins and outs of irony," I say. "I'm in Mom's breasts."

She agrees to meet me at a museum in the city. In the lobby, a well-dressed man hanging an umbrella on a museum-provided hanger activates a dull ache in my subletted pelvis. I compartmentalize this thought as I exchange pleasantries with the woman selling tickets. The fantasy refuses to yield and to my horror unfurls in detail. A bluish hotel room, smoke from cigarettes, his full ass, sliding my underwear down. Is this me or my mother? I like sex but am not prone to vivid fantasy in the middle of the day. I don't want to be in the mental room as she daydreams, yet I'm swept along as the fantasy persists. I step into the first room of photographs wanting to do the equivalent of boil my brain.

This is when the eggs re-announce themselves in my gut. In front of a Crewdson photo, my stomach roils and flips. My mother farts. A loud, certain sound, so unexpected I laugh, alone in the room. It settles my stomach. It is intoxicating how satisfying this is. I push to see if I can do it again. But the force needs time to gather. The tang reaches me so I move to another room where a couple leans into an illuminated box where a suburban family sits at a breakfast table. The father spreads margarine onto a roll. The mother passes the daughter a saltshaker. A cartoon sun hangs over the house. The lawn is dotted with toys. The deckle-edged scene is meant to appear ripped from a magazine.

My stomach activates and she farts again. I glare at the woman, feigning shock. She looks to her partner with alarm as I leave the room.

Eggs, body, room-clearing gas. Mother.

Daguerreotype portraits line the hallway. A college-age student is on my observing schedule. If he notices my discomfort, it doesn't alter his course. We remain in step until the last photo, a bouquet of dead flowers.

I leave the student and move to the final room, meant to be an exclamation point at the end of the exhibit. It is empty, thank god, because my mother's stomach is building to climax. A fart issues from me with such force I have to brace against a table of fake brochures. I am so ashamed that tears grow. Mother, what do you go through? The man from the lobby enters. His handsome coat fits him well. He crosses to the far side of the room as if sensing my need for privacy. A gentleman. But he stands between me and the door and I need to get my mother to the bathroom. The man examines a photorealistic painting of Robert Redford. He doesn't notice my agony. Robert Redford doesn't do anything but shine. We are all three trapped in this moment together.

A new movement elicits a sound like a child whining from my stomach. My mother's pain ceases. I am overcome by exhaustion like the end of a working day. The man is surprised. He'd been coming over to talk, I guess.

As I limp past, his lips retract over his teeth. His face grows pained.

I lead my mother down the shallow flight of stairs to the sanctuary of the lobby bathroom and lock us in a stall where we rest. I realize I've become her caretaker as empathy unrolls inside me. How has she been handling planning my wedding amid the dissolution of her own marriage? It must have been difficult raising us weird kids alone. It must have been agony when I was injured. When who she thought was her son turned away. This generosity of spirit is unwelcome. I want to continue to disregard her. But her limbs are so heavy, the heart under the borrowed rib cage craving honesty like the rest of us. I can't help but feel closer to her.

"I'm sorry, Mom," I tell her.

My sister waits in the lobby. Seeing me, her eyes widen and she takes several steps back.

"It's me," I beg.

"Prove it."

I cover my face. "She has horrible gas and she's horny, Simone. She had a full-on sexual fantasy about a man in there. She's humiliating me. I have to go to the emergency room."

"Let's get some water." She leads me to a bench and pulls a bottle from her bag. She watches as I sip. "If you're in there, where's Mom?"

"She's in here somewhere, being muffled. I know it's her because she's disparaging me."

"Sooner or later every woman wakes up and realizes she is her mother."

"Simone. Help."

My phone rings. It is the groom. "Put it on speaker," Simone says.

"Darling," he says. "I got your message but I don't have time for theatrics. I have news that isn't bad and isn't good. It's powerful in the long-term, depending on how you see it."

"Something has happened," I say.

"Something has," he admits. "The Board wants me to come in. I'll get time over and another half. Which is good for us."

Relief distracts me. I won't have to see him until the following night.

"I'll get there in time for the groom's dinner," he says. "I hope everything there is okay."

"Everything here is on fire."

He gives his warm chuckle, my humor lets him off the hook. "I'll be there tomorrow night and put out all your fires then."

My fires. Theatrics. "You're right," I say. "Big deal out of nothing."

"Get a massage. Take a bath." A female voice asks him a sharp question. "My meeting is here. Gotta go. I love love love you." The phone disconnects.

Simone says, "He sounds . . . I can't think of the word."

Museumgoers collect in the lobby to wait out a sudden storm. Simone, my mother, and I watch through giant windows. Trees shake. The weeping against the windows intensifies. The wind makes the evergreen gesture to itself. Points down and over there, over there. A wind gust makes the branches give a collective wave. The tree stills, as if the entire courtyard is thinking. Then the wind kicks up and the tree points to itself again. The lightning glimmers and vanishes. Pauses, glimmers. Me, says the narcissist tree. Now, you. That guy. That guy and me. The storm abates. Short time coming, short time gone. We watch the sky, still gray with light growing behind it of some future, sunny day. This is the most we've done together in years. A family, kind of.

Simone studies me/our mother. "She's still wearing her hair like the wife of a Midwest preacher, like she has since her thirties. She must have loved that age."

"Isn't that when she was pregnant with you?"

"Let's get out of here," Simone says. "I hate museums."

The rain has downgraded to a suggestion as we move our mother down the misted street. I try to avoid my reflection in the windows we pass but I can't help looking at her disembodied ghosts of hands. The existential ramifications set in and my breathing worsens. The rain falls again.

"Do you still want to go to a hospital?" Simone says. "There's one nearby."

"What would I tell them? Hello, I'm not myself today."

"Patient complains of elderly vagina."

My phone rings.

"You're fifteen minutes late!" the florist yells. "Your consistent thoughtlessness is almost admirable!"

"Do you want to pick up a bouquet with me?" I ask Simone.

"No." She puts on a delicate pair of sunglasses and says we've been in this Beckett catastrophe for too long without food. Being with her levels me, the smooth way she meets chaos with style, matches gazes with questioning men on the street.

We find a restaurant and order one martini and two steaks.

"It's my mother's birthday," Simone tells the waiter. "She's turning one hundred. Can we have free cake?" She turns to me. "You should have ordered her a salad. You're out of shape, old lady." She's having fun criticizing our mother in front of her face.

I lift my dress and show her the thighs. I grab a handful and shake.

"Please put those away. I would like to eat again."

Mother craves rye. Mother craves the men at the bar who throw soldierlike nods. The heaviness in mother's bones spreads. She has to go to bed soon. The dark voice says, rest, idiot.

"Mom and I both have the slut gene," I say. "She's pulled toward every man."

"I don't enjoy that thought." Simone discards the potatoes from her plate onto a napkin she slides over to me, a leftover tradition from childhood that pleases me.

Later, I blow out a sputtering candle on a cupcake.

"This is the first birthday I've had with Mom as an adult," I say.

"Look at us," Simone says. "Have you ever seen such fucked-up sisters?"

"Sisters." I smile.

We pay the check, stand on the sidewalk, and say goodbye for the second time in as many days. The wedding guests will arrive the following night, and I'll have to go to the hospital to take care of this mother aneurysm. Simone knows I'm falling into myself and tries lightness. "You have Mom whiskers," she says. "What are you going to do?"

"I wish I knew," I say.

"I'm sorry but I can't hug you in that form."

"I wouldn't want to hug me either."

"She never did, did she? Hug us." She turns to leave. "Call if you need anything."

"I never got to say goodbye to him," I say. My needs are like a child's, narrow and selfish.

She sighs. Above our heads a dress is being yanked across the street on a clothing line. We watch until a set of hands pulls it into a window. I think she will say no, but then she places a hand on my shoulder. "All right. Say it."

I close my eyes. "Tom," I say. "Goodbye."

"Goodbye."

"Do you have anything you'd like to say to Mom?" I joke.

Her expression remains humorless. "No."

"I wish you could come to the wedding," I say.

She says, "I wish the whole world was different."

We turn and walk in opposite directions. I miss her immediately.

The hotel lobby is empty when I return. In my room, I lay my mother's body onto the bed. The phone rings. *Please be her.*

Simone says, "Were you serious about Granny visiting you?"

I tell her about the toothpaste, the shoddy elevator, arriving in the suddenly aviated room, the bird, the question about the Internet ("Not bad," she says, about my explanation), the bellboy who hates birds, Granny's request, the wedding dress, the doppelgänger ("There is no Northeast Fourth Street in Brooklyn," she says), the husband. As I speak her gentle mmm-hmmms tick off every point.

"Why me?" she says when the story is finished. "Why now?" I don't know, I say, and she says she doesn't know either.

"Sometimes a cigar is just a cigar," I say.

"Where was she when I went through everything? I could have used a bird, some guidance."

A pang of doom. Everything I said the night before led to walls. There must be a way to approach her so that she'll trust that even if I'm flawed, I have good intentions. "How can I love you?" I say. "Best. How can I love you best?"

Her tone softens. She says, "One of the women I was at the clinic with, a farm girl from Minnesota, was so delighted to finally be herself, had supportive parents even, holding her hand through all the shots. The surgeries. She moves to the city and she's finally living. Meets a guy on Tinder who figures out who she is and strangles her. That was a friend of mine. It's like getting on a plane to fly home. And you're so excited. But the plane never lands. So you're just always trying to get there."

It is the gentlest movement of a days-long conversation. I lie on the comforter in the unlit room with my eyes closed, receiver pressed against my ear, listening to her tender voice. She tells me she was obsessed with Shakespeare because of the disguises. A man dressed as a woman dressed as a man presents himself to the king. As themselves, the characters are out of sorts, incorrect. But in disguise, they feel most like themselves. "Of course, I didn't know that's why I was drawn to Shakespeare," she says. "I just thought I liked the tights."

I tell her I loved the groom deeply and painfully at first, then remember I am speaking to someone who can understand life's complications. "That's not true. I never did. I wanted to. He said commitment is as simple as yes or no. Either we date or we don't stay friends. I said okay and waited for passion to come."

"Did it?"

Once through the coffee shop window I watched a woman say goodbye to her girlfriend. She was leaving for work, or maybe they didn't live in the same city. They held each other and spoke quietly. I'll be back, she was saying. It won't be long. They didn't conceal their tears, the sorrow too big to stay private. What's a long time, anyway? If you want to understand how vast two minutes can be, ask anyone separated from their love. Let that be me, I begged myself. Let his absence cancel breath. I tell Simone I can't imagine crying that way about the groom. The distance between what I was supposed to feel and what I actually felt grew. It opened windows in me, and the windows let the birds in.

"It's just like Granny to shit on everything."

"Literally," I say. "We missed out on so many jokes. Being

estranged. I've been so anxious for so long. Rose says it's in my head."

"You've always trusted her too much."

"Still," I say. "Aren't I supposed to be happy?"

"Messy is honest. Fine," she says, "is the word I was looking for. He seems fine."

"I think the sun is up," I say though I don't check, and she says, "Here, too."

"When Gregor Samsa woke up as a bug," I say, "it was about being useless to society."

She says, "What's more societally useless than a woman in her seventies?"

This launches us into broad, sweeping laughter, mine in gusts and hers more contained, chugging underneath. I hear the aluminum hum of waves, or maybe steel cars on the highway furred by distance, I climb to reach a windowsill and find myself already over, her voice is the clasped hand pulling me to safety over and over until I don't know if I'm speaking aloud or if my thoughts are movements and earnest knocking wakes me.

Through the peephole I see a pot of anxious lilies held by the bellboy who is scared of birds ("Good morning," he says, fearfully). I open the door, dig through my pockets for a dollar. "I'll find my wallet."

I pass in front of the hallway mirror and catch sight of my mussed hair and blurred face. My hair. My face.

The wallet slips my grasp and lands on the carpet. I test my arms and legs, enjoying the lightness. It's as if I've been relieved of my skin and am a spirit. I reach, bend, lunge.

"Ma'am?" the bellboy says.

"Look at me!" I say, in tears. "I'm not my mother anymore!"

He references the hallway for escape but whether the employees of this hotel like it or not, all of this week's enormous changes have occurred in front of them.

"What is your name?" I lean in, anticipating an important, serendipitous moniker.

"James," he says.

"James." I am disappointed. "I don't know anyone named that."

"Okay." He wants to leave, a reasonable thought in an unreasonable hotel room. I pull a bill from my wallet.

"Do you go by Jim?" I say.

He pockets the bill. "Just James."

The lilies are from Aunt Henshaw, who has a tendency to summarize whatever's going on in unsurprising ways. The note: *You are getting married soon.* After James leaves I return to my sister on the phone. "Are you there?"

"Barely," she says. "I fell asleep."

"I'm myself again," I say. "Me. My self."

"Show me. Send a selfie."

"I hate selfies."

"See your way clear to making an exception this once."

I take a picture and message it to her. She is quiet for so long I ask if she's received it. "Seeing you. I forgot. You're beautiful. You're so," she says, "brown. No one else looks like you."

"Better than Mom, right?"

She doesn't want to joke. "I'd show your picture to the doctors," she says. "I'd tell them, as close to her as possible. Simone was the name of my friend who was killed."

I make a noise, a protracted oh, as what feels like a million tiny birds I didn't realize were sitting on my chest fly away.

I stand naked in front of the bathroom mirror, admiring the tuft of cirrus curls that insist around my neck, my shoulders, slim arms, breasts like discouraged lowercase *j*'s topped with hard tips, the roundness of my belly that complements my hips, black pubic hair I groom with a slim pair of scissors, the generous thighs pocked with cellulite, the paunchy ass that sometimes does well in jeans but most times does not, even the gummed scars that mark my right knee, thigh and hip and torso, on a topographical map these marks would signify a mountain range, once a stranger shoved a knife into me like he was putting it back where it belonged the way you'd cram a book onto a loaded shelf, and the skin over all of it an unending reply the color of coffee and nicotine, things I like, things that are fine in small doses but dangerous in large quantities. I cup my hip bones, savoring their hardness against my palms.

Welcome back, I say to myself.

Thinking of my grandmother, I dial my mother. *A bird today,* she said. *Myself again tomorrow*. My mother answers on the second ring. "What's wrong?"

"Nothing's wrong. How are you feeling, Mother?"

"You're just calling?"

A noise behind her like ice in a glass. My stepfather asks, "Who is it?"

"Do you need something? Is he here?"

"Is who here?"

"The groom, of course!"

After the loving conversation with Simone, my mother's words sound unusually sharp. Yet I've intimately encountered the private voice that threatens her. "I'm only calling to say hello, to make sure you have everything you need."

"Everything I need," she says, like it's a riddle. My good intention wilts. "I've prayed to your grandparents for sun tomorrow. If the weather's bad, blame them."

"I like rain," I say. "Mother," I say. "How can I love you best?" It's shameful to use the same trick twice but I do it.

From the Inn's cavernous expanse, far enough away that I can't tell if it's above or below me, I hear an unmistakable, overly dramatic *Achoo*.

"Are you on drugs?" my mother says.

The empathy box slams shut. "Yes. And drunk. I'm several bottles of wine in and smoked a ton of weed."

"Aunt Henshaw is complaining again." She sounds relieved I have returned us to our roles: me the insufferable, she the put-upon. "We'll need a pillow for her chair."

"Who is it?" my stepfather insists.

"Don't be late," she says. "Wear the green."

"Sorry to bother," I say, but she's already hung up.

I stare at the receiver in my hand, benevolence deleted, embarrassed by my good intentions and ashamed for an amorphous reason I can't explain. This comes as a relief—it is the way I always feel after we speak.

I consider what it would take to bring the wedding to a halt. The Inn, the baker, the waiters, the florist. Would it irreparably damage the tether connecting me to others? Can I articulate the wrongness well enough to make everyone laugh, saying, "Your mother, farting!" Liquid sloshing in cocktail glasses until I tucked into mental bed each person I'd inconvenienced, assured that there was no better option than to discard thousands of dollars of our parents' money? I cannot. Yet I also cannot imagine the fabric of my life containing both things: my sister folding her hands on her lap (the future) and the groom eating a sandwich and watching a baseball game (the past). Outside a bird chirps, *Call it off.* No, it is children playing.

When we met, the stubble on his jawline and above his ears in his close shave was like down, I wanted to make a coat out of him.

He touches me so gently, I told my friends.

Until one day I realized, he doesn't. In fact, he hurls himself at me. I have to brace, waiting for the pummel. What made me think he was gentle? I fought this new idea, refusing to believe I'd been wrong. In bed I asked if he would touch me like he used to. And he said what I'd been fearing, "I'm doing the same thing I always have." He wasn't malicious. He was confused. It was I who was mistaken.

The next night he pulled away then advanced in a performative way. I thought he was soothing a muscle kink, but he did it again. It was some kind of physical system, shying away from himself then moving into me again. He said, "I'm doing what you asked."

He thought that's what it meant to be tender, retreat and advance, retreat and advance.

▲ ▼ ▲

I craft emoji-rich responses to brunch invitations, remember paper towels, who likes artichokes, then remember deeper: I deliver hellos, concoct opportunities for his intelligence to shine. I am a Post-it. If you do these things while pocketing a part of yourself, if you complete the correct actions with the mental equivalent of a caveat, who is the person engaging in the action, and who is left behind? Fiancée, a location between two states of being. I am no longer what I was. Yet I am not quite. This is a hyphen of time, an antechamber.

The groom does not deserve to have a wife with a retreating soul. I do not deserve to be gripped in place each time I want to leap. I will go through with the wedding, our life. He will come home from school, I will come home from interviewing clients. We will watch television and grill slabs of chicken. It is not the chicken's fault, or society's, or the meticulous florist's, or the groom's, that I've led us all onto Long Island to witness the beginning of what everyone hopes will be a happy marriage. On what everyone hopes will be a clear day. Everyone has prayed to their ancestors for good weather. If there's sun, the dead will be praised and, on the occasion of rain, blamed.

THE GROOM, OF COURSE!

Raise high the roofbeam, carpenters. The groom walks meekly down the hall. I hear the characteristic sound of a throat being cleared that does not need to be, then a polite "Excuse me," though he is alone, fumbling with the card in the door.

He enters the room, holding an arrangement of lilacs and Queen Anne's lace: my bouquet. It is wilder and larger than I expected, the decision of a woman who craves attention. I hate it immediately.

"The florist called," he says. "She was in a state."

"So thoughtful of you to pick it up." We hug and for a moment I am calmed by his familiar, stable bones under my grip. His thoughtfulness.

"I hit a median in the parking lot but it's okay." He says, "I'll take the car in on Monday to check it out." He is still speaking to the me I was earlier in the week, who hadn't yet encountered her avian grandmother, fought herself and lost, been sistered, occupied space within her mother.

As I dress he navigates through channels on the television,

calling out updates. The Henshaws are here. His parents have arrived. Then, "Do you think we could have sex tonight?" His voice is quiet. "It would be nice."

"It's the night before our wedding," I say.

"I'm so glad." He starts his electric toothbrush, shuts it off. "You are so hot." The toothbrush hums across his molars as he switches to a ball game. The canned multitude of a crowd and an announcer proclaims, "Higher and higher, another victory." The groom's gums buzz.

"I have to go down to the front desk to borrow a hair dryer," I say.

"Isn't there one right here?" He yanks it from the wall, shows it to me.

"I need," I say, "another one."

I take a back staircase to a door leading outside. I sit in the gazebo and spend a long time looking at the lake. In the lobby, the concierge performs the hmmms and okays that signal the end of a phone call and smiles to let me know I'm her priority as soon as she's finished.

"Me again," I say.

"How's that toothpaste treating you?"

I show her my teeth and she gives me a thumbs-up. "Our hair dryer broke," I lie.

"I think we have one in the back." She leaves to get it.

"I forgot to ask," I say when she returns. "How old is your daughter?"

"Seven." She says the number as if it contains magic. "She lives with me for most of the week but spends weekends with her dad in the city."

"You must hate to be without her."

"You have no idea," she says.

I ask if she likes the current movie every little girl in America is wild over. "Can't stop dancing to it," she says. "Me and her father didn't work out but she's a good kid."

"Most times it's for the best," I say.

"It is with us. He's a good guy, but two control freaks in one house is too many. She's an angel, despite it all. And I'd say if she was a jerk. Is your husband finding everything okay?"

"Fiancé," I say. "Yes."

"He just arrived?"

"Yes," I say. "His job takes him away a lot. Even for his wedding."

"Now it's my turn. You must hate to be without him."

There is a scrambling sound in the vicinity of the elevator where people have disembarked. The concierge and I turn to see a well-dressed older couple. The man wears a navy suit. The woman is layered in shiny materials the color of lamb or something else easily slaughtered, a blood-colored pin accuses out from her lapel.

"There she is," my mother says. "What is she doing? Doesn't she know she's late? That everyone is already seated and waiting for her to arrive? Is she even dressed? Is this what she's going to wear? Didn't we agree on the green?"

This is the first time I've seen her since I was her. My stepfather dodders behind, posture arranged in its familiar apologies-in-advance. The concierge and I are still blinking in the pleasant afterthought of her daughter, an angel despite it all.

I say, "Are we talking to me?"

My stepfather leaves to tell the others they've found me. My mother pulls a small package from her purse. "A gift," she says.

Inside, a tiny locket is pinned to delicate fabric. She opens it to reveal a picture of my grandmother, gazing into middle distance beyond the photographer's shoulder, unimpressed, mouth poised to criticize. The other side is empty. "You can put a picture from the wedding there. You and the groom."

I fold her into a hug she does not appreciate. She smells like piles of tea towels in the sun. "Okay," she says, sounding upset.

I release her. "Are you well, Mother? Are you enjoying the Inn? The eggs," I say, ". . . have been particularly good. I want you to know that I appreciate the money you've put into this wedding, and how difficult it must have been to raise us. Essentially alone."

"It was fine," she says, distracted by a noise on the other side of the lobby.

I hold the locket out. "She looks aggravated."

My mother nods. "I didn't have many pictures to choose from."

"Do you ever talk to her?"

"Your grandmother? She's dead."

"I realize that. But did you ever try? Say hello. Yell at her even."

"That sort of thing doesn't occur to me. We were never what you'd call close," she admits. "She always wanted me to be more cheerful."

My laughter embarrasses her. She smooths her hair and checks who's watching.

"That's almost punk rock," I say. "Very goth, Mom."

"I didn't know I was able to make you laugh," she says.

"You make me laugh."

"Not like your brother. Tom was the one to get you howling."

She notices more than I realize. His name, no longer attached to anyone, moves through the room like a haunting, like the bellboy rolling a table into the elevator where he will no doubt get stuck for hours.

My mother and I stand in the lobby, thinking of my brother. I decide to be honest. "I wish he was here."

She says, "I wish everyone was here so we could eat."

The groom's aunt Henshaw bursts from the dining room in mid-conversation with a person who does not appear. She says she's not doing well, sciatica, bad neighbors, joint pain, you name it. She says, "Sometimes I feel like I get older every day."

I instantly hear how Simone would answer, *That's the way it works, old lady*, but I say, "I know what you mean. Some mornings I wake up and I'm a hundred years old."

She nods. "It's like every day, more and more time passes."

My mother and Aunt Henshaw retreat into the dining room. I realize the concierge has been waiting.

"Guess I'll go," I say. "Though I'd rather stay and chat."

We smile at each other.

"I forgot to tell you," she says. "We fixed the elevator!"

"No more bird guts clogging everything up?" She hadn't said anything about bird guts, but she participates.

"No more guts," she says. "That bird was a mess but we got it out. Well, James did."

"But James hates birds," I say.

"Sometimes we have to do what we hate?"

"To that end." I jerk a thumb toward the dining room.

"I thought you could rest easier knowing you can rely on our elevator."

After a few more go-arounds of gratitude, I enter the dining room of flickering candles where everything is golden, wine-charmed, and near, as if the room hovers above itself.

Seated are many important players of the wedding: the groom, forking shrimp out of a festive glass. Rose, swaddled in a gleaming pashmina. My mother, pointing to my stepfather. The groom's mother and father, white-haired, meant for the top of a cake, dignitaries of impressive meringue. We pass plates of luminous meat to one another. After dinner, people excuse themselves to the bathroom or out for smokes. Vacancies occur, people move from table to table, visiting.

I turn to the groom. "Before we marry, there's something you should know."

He moves closer so I can speak into the area of his folded collar. I'm grateful for his cilantro-and-club-chair smell.

Weeks before, thick slices of fondant and sponge had been placed in front of us on trays. We were to choose one for our wedding cake. One confection was presented with more ceremony than the others.

"Vanilla almond," the woman said, "with lemon basil icing."

"The bride does not like almond," the groom said proudly. To have a bride and to know what she doesn't like.

But the woman anticipated this. "Not a problem," she said. "You can't even taste it."

"A client once invited me to his house for a party," I tell him. "He was the young musician injured while walking. I thought I'd only stay for half an hour, but I ended up having fun. After midnight it was only me and him and his core friends. They decided to have a dance party to an obscure band." I pause, noting his confusion. "Christopher? Who loved to walk and was hit by a texting single mother? I stayed for the dancing. I didn't know anyone else liked that band let alone a whole roomful of people. I chatted outside with one of his roommates. He was sweet. I took him home. The next morning the subways were closed so I drove him back to where the party had been. There was a hurricane coming and I didn't want to be stuck with him. Then the hurricane came."

I remember the silence before the storm, the eggy light after, the couple I knew from college who'd been injured by a falling tree.

Guests return.

"Speech," a cousin yells.

"I forgive you," the groom says.

"Speech," from my stepfather.

"For what?" I say.

"Sleeping with a client's roommate."

"Forgiveness is not the reason I'm telling you this story. I won't ever be able to arrive at a party of strangers and fuck a young man again. It's not about the fucking, it's about the feeling free. Doesn't that worry you?"

He chortles, a benevolent sound that cheers me. I believe he will comfort me. "Not at all."

"Speech," Rose says. Aunt Henshaw, the cousins. My mother returns from the bathroom, furious with the contents of her pocketbook, and joins the chorus.

Someone tosses the groom a microphone. "Speech," he says. The amplification startles him, he hands it to me.

"I've been thinking a lot about being wedded, which is good, you know, as I'm about to be wedded. I get the sense the number of people who are married is not equal to the number that give the institution much thought. Am I curious enough? Antonia, remember the time you asked so many questions about the beer's hoppiness that the bartender finally poured samples of everything on draft? Yet how many questions do we ask before we get married? We proceed into this institution with nary a curiosity. Let alone an entire flight. So many people assume it's a step we're entitled to take. It's difficult to unlearn all that water. I'm referencing that parable about a fish who was asked, *What is it like to breathe underwater?*

"I spent a week with a woman in Chicago, waking up and finding coffee and sitting at movies we chose together. She had a husband, a family. I had a life in New York. It was a stolen season. But she was some kind of wife to me.

"Rose's grandmother spent forty years with Rose's grandfather and told me she never liked him. Forty years with a partner she stayed with because she never had to go too deep. She said one day a certain light fell on him as he reached for a box on the top shelf and she felt a new jolt. Love, maybe. After forty years, the marriage begins.

"One of my clients has dementia and has fallen in love with her own son. She's hot for him, can't wait to be close, asks him: 'Why did you leave me?' You tell me that isn't real, abiding. Marriage, of a sort.

"There's a four-paneled painting of goldfish in L.A.'s Chinatown that I love, the fish swim in their separate panels, lonely and happy, and maybe that's why my mind is on that analogy I'm possibly misremembering. In any case, *What's water?* That's what the fish replies when he's asked: *What is it like to breathe underwater?*

"Does everyone love in a different way, like flavors? Mine is pistachio and someone else's is chocolate cereal? Am I able to love stronger and more deliberately on command, or can love only be elicited? Are there limits? Are we born with a finite amount or is our capacity infinite? I'd bet that depends on the die you're tossed around with and end up on the table next to. Chance. Is there a way to sharpen and refine love? And all the variations between the variations? If there is, I'd like to. Or I'd absolutely not like to. I'd like to know more about it before I decide.

"You're all nice people and I'm sorry I did this to you."

The groom takes the microphone out of my hand. "My future wife," he says, flushing as everyone applauds. "Always with the questions."

On most days, beauty goes unremarked upon in these people's lives, but on nights like this they say: I am delighted to be here. Their happiness draws a line underneath me. I am sad in a happy place. With every exultation of gratitude, I retreat until my body sits on a chair at a table, but my soul is pressed into one of the corners, struggling to breathe. The problem with the room is that it's gorgeous and shining but people are missing.

I cross the lobby to the elevator, get in, and press the button. Between floors, I crank the emergency release, call Simone, and watch myself in the mirror leave a minutes-long message.

"I want you to know," I say, then stall. I've just said the word *love* a dozen times yet find myself unable to utter it into her voice mail. "Please come to the wedding tomorrow. It's not right you won't be there. We won't tell anyone. You'll sit in the back. Come as a woman disguised as a man. We'll *Twelfth Night* the shit out of everyone. You said yourself how easy it is for a middle-aged woman to disappear. Please. I don't want to do this alone." Before I hang up I say, "This is your mother."

"Is everything all right?" The concierge's voice drifts through the speaker.

"You really need to get this elevator under control." I swipe tears from my cheeks. "Enough is enough. I'm trying to understand," I say. "I'm doing my best."

"We know you're trying and we appreciate it."

"One person can only be so forgiving."

"You've gone out of your way," the voice agrees.

"How hard is it to get someone to fix this thing for real? James or whoever."

The voice sounds like it's crying. "We're sorry," it says. "We don't mean to ruin anything."

"Now I'm supposed to feel bad because you're crying?"

"No. We did this to ourselves."

"You did," I say. "Making your bed and all. Lying in it."

"We're resetting it. You'll be down in a jiffy."

"A jiffy." I curse.

The reset elevator descends to the lobby. The doors open to

reveal my family in hues of tipsiness. Seeing me they quack with delight, join me on the elevator. Everyone is thrilled. The groom and I return to our room where I remove my jewelry and clothes. He pulls down his underwear and chucks it with his toe. The graying hair against the paleness of his chest always surprises me, as opposed to mine, dark on dark. He tells me he's been working out for me and I say he looks great, but I wish there were more of him, that even my widest embrace couldn't hold all of him. He places his hands on my hips and positions me next to him.

"Your skin." He kisses my shoulder. "I've missed it."

"I called all week," I say. "Where were you? There were things I wanted to talk to you about."

He stops, aggravation dusts his smile. "I'm here now, aren't I?"

Yes, I say, because he is due for it, and I've promised. We don't have sex often because his work makes him tired. I like this because it allows us to ignore other, bigger problems.

He appreciates everything as he climbs me: thighs, stomach, breasts. There is nothing technically wrong with how he touches me. He's not strong enough to plank above me so he props himself on one elbow. From that fortified position, he enters me.

My subconscious has at least ten working, active planes. One conducts everyday business, hands money to the ticket girl. Designs appropriate responses to banal conversations. On the daydream plane I receive an award for courage, take my seat, am called onstage to receive it again. On another, an endless film of regrets: I refuse the childhood girl who wanted to be friends because her ugliness scared me. A boy gifts me tickets to a concert to which I take another boy. In the childhood plane my mother looks up at my entrance to a room and her expression remains unchanged.

The list-of-worries plane: climate change, terrorist attack. The rerun-of-great-sex plane—pulled hair, he holds me in a straddling position while he stands. Napping with my child-hood dog. My mother looks up at my entrance into a room, her expression unchanged. One plane intones random phrases: THE BRIDE DOES NOT LIKE ALMOND. YOU COULD BRAISE BEEF IN MILK, I SUPPOSE.

YOU ARE HAVING SEX, says the practical plane, to remind me of the body, both mine and the one moving part of itself farther into me. I'm pleased he is close to orgasm and hope it will be over soon.

One plane, buried in the underground layers, works on philosophical tangles like what it meant when Rose said, "Don't worry about me." Conclusions I'm not ready for are secreted in deeper planes. The upturned-penny plane tries positive out-comes: promotion, connection to nature. My mother looks up at my entrance to a room.

YOU ARE HAVING SEX.

My clients' injuries have destroyed many of these planes. A meteor careens through the framework of a skyscraper, shear-ing the beams in half. Thoughts halt in the middle. The structure sways. Only Danny's literal plane remains. He is no longer funny. Post-its act as surrogates.

YOU ARE MAKING RICE.

Danny in his gently pulsing room of Post-its, and good sex, and how I should have gone with the boy who gave me the tick-ets, and said yes to the girl, the career of Ewan McGregor with its nebulous ebbs and flows. Like the Internet, simultaneous and indifferent. I shake back into my body and the groom comes into me, eyes wide and focused on the headboard.

He gives me a satisfied snarl. The phone rings.

"You're going to get that?" he says. "You never answer your phone."

On the other end a frantic woman asks if I'm there. "It's Clover," she says. "Danny's wife." She pauses and the details of her return to me: she borrows Danny's meds to sleep, hair box-dyed a color called Spring Break. "I came from the hospital," she says. "I was at the house earlier. Danny's lunch was staying down, which I took as a good sign. He had a bug all week. The doctor said something was going around."

The groom slides out of bed and crosses to the bathroom in the pallid light.

It is not uncommon for clients' relatives to call to relay simple things like they would in a diary. "Clover?" I say. "Are you okay?"

"I came back from my meeting and he told me my sister had called. I think he wanted me to be on the phone when he . . ."

The groom curses in the bathroom, a dropped metal thing. I have a sister now, too, I think. To Clover, I say, "When he what?"

"He waited until I was on the phone," she says. "I guess he thought that'd be a good way for him to."

"For him to what?"

"For him to. He shot himself."

She describes the smell of burning, the smear of blood still on her. The groom draws the curtains, revealing the lake and sky. I clamber under the sheets, still naked. Thousands of miles above, a plane glides out from a bank of navy clouds. Clover says, the nurses. The name of the hospital. The plane reveals itself again. I think of the passengers, feet swinging over plastic seats, watching movie screens above the city's grid. The conflation of tin and sky. For a moment, Danny is a small thing seen from thousands of miles above. I'm not certain I know him or the woman on the phone who is overcome with tears. I tell her I'll come to the hospital and hang up.

"One of my clients shot himself," I say. "He's at the hospital."

"He's alive?" the groom says.

"No," I say.

He frowns. "If he's dead, he wouldn't be at the hospital."

"He was still alive when they . . . Is this the fucking point?"

"I don't know why I'm arguing. I'm sorry."

I pull my dress on and fasten the important buttons, leaving the subsidiary ones for the elevator. "I'm going."

"You can't. It's the night before our wedding."

I lace my boots. "I'll take a car. I won't be long."

"At least give me a hug," he says.

I lean against him, he pulls me in. "My hardworking girl. So dedicated to the most vulnerable among us." There are moments when he says the right thing so convincingly I can't believe him.

"It sounds like you're running for office," I say.

"You're a mean girl."

I appreciate this honesty and think about it. I still think about it.

I sit in Coney Island Hospital answering a police officer's questions. Morning sun makes the waiting room appear basted. A room before a room.

She asks how long I've been seeing Danny and if he'd displayed suicidal tendencies. I say he had to remove his feces with his own gloved hands. She studies me through a pair of reading glasses. "What is your job exactly?"

I tell her I map pain, which is not unlike aging, in that it is characterized by what we can no longer do. For most people, aging is doing less and less. It's not the pain, I explain to the officer, it is the actions pain makes impossible. Those of us who are healthy should use our bodies as much as we can, I tell her. Threesomes, foursomes, moresomes. Detecting nothing useful in my story, she leaves.

Clover enters and we exchange a stiff hug. We sit on hard chairs and talk.

"I rushed him during our last appointment," I say. "Did he mention? That I was weird?"

"Don't blame yourself," she says. "It's his fault. And mine. He'd threatened to do it before when we fought."

She looks blurred by shock, blinking to bring me and the room into focus.

"I'm beginning to think the dead are never really gone." I want to say something helpful. "That they visit in different ways. Glints of snow on a mountain. Tea in a cup."

"I don't believe in that," she says.

"I don't either."

And yet.

On my way out of the hospital I stop to pet R2-D2, leashed to a bench down the hall. Light coming from a surgical room makes his fur glow. He's never run in a field. No one has ever tossed him a ball. He stares, alert, into a room I can't see.

The cop leans against the nurses' station filling out paperwork. "What happens to the dog?" I say.

It takes the cop a moment to figure out the animal I mean. She shrugs. "He'll be taken to the shelter. The wife doesn't want him."

R2-D2's tail wags. He sniffs happily around my ankles. The world's mistreated things are still optimistic despite it all. The Coney Island shelter is understaffed and badly maintained. I've stopped in occasionally to visit the birds. "You'll find a good home," I tell him. The nurses at their station, heads tilted into their paperwork. The jaundiced light of illness.

Outside, the wind gains strength from the ocean and I lift my collar against whatever can be blocked. There's been a rhythm in my head for days. A wordless, tuneless heart beating alongside my actions. It goes: Boom. Boom boom. An elevator song? Boom. Boom boom. Then I realize. It is my grandmother saying, *Oh. He's white.*

It's morning and Saturday, technically. I will be married

today. At Shop and Save I search for the friendliest-seeming sleeve of peonies. Holding it, I practice. "I'm so, so, so," I say. ". . . excited."

In the checkout line, I scan the magazines. A celebrity is sad, pregnant. I allow myself to think of Tom for the length of the wait. No matter how wrong or putrid, fucked up or sad, no one except him could make me laugh until my abs ache. He was the least boring person. It was too painful to bear witness to his misery when he was addicted. I think of him in heels, taupe control-top tights, twisting the waistband of his skirt to correct its alignment like women do. The full measure of fluorescent supermarket light hits my thoughts. She is happy. Hard knots shake loose in my shoulders. *Happy*: like white rice, the word comes with every meal, but in reality, happiness is so elusive it may as well be supernatural. I drag my items down the tacky checkout line. The woman in front of me pays for the makings of a solo dinner and enough food for one adored cat. I'm jealous of whomever gets to see Simone regularly and would pay any amount, wound anyone, skip anything, for a quotidian day with her.

"What beautiful flowers." The cashier punches numbers into the machine. "Special occasion?"

"I'm getting married today."

He is so rapturous that for a moment I believe I've said the wrong thing. He's being dramatic and sincere. "I hope I get to do that one day."

"Get your flowers at Shop and Save?"

"No, silly." He wraps the peonies in brown paper. "Get married."

"Marriage is not an achievement," I say for what feels like the tenth time. No one can imagine an ambivalent bride. Except, I remember, Peaseblossom the parakeet, who hated weddings.

The young actor has won. This, plus the cashier's delight, makes me bratty and capable of damage. I will punch this display of protein powders, I think, but instead I remain silent as tears arrive.

"You're so happy!" he says. "Look at you, crying!"

He hands the flowers to me and says good luck. As I fold bills into my wallet, he tells a girl wearing the unflattering company apron, "She's getting married today. So happy she's crying."

"Enjoy!" Her tone implies that she wishes something for me, but whatever it is does not include joy. She and Peaseblossom are sisters in dismay. *Enjoy*: the enthusiasm equivalent of *Congrats*.

Those of us jumpy, sensitive, injured, maligned, gaslit as shit, disappeared, panicky, bullied, skin-thin, hyperspecific, de-spined, poorly drugged, weak-willed, fetishized, micro-assaulted, truck-dragged, browbeat insomnimaniacs with unfair bowels and role models, life-ruining kink addictions, and piss-poor familial connections, haremed and hoovered, sealed screaming into closets and shoved under love seats find it hard enough to ease our scraped brains into the compact-only parking spot at the Shop and Save let alone into anything resembling peace without someone threatening, *Enjoy!*

I match her blankness. "Thank you."

I decide to take the train back to Long Island. The F roars into the station and my reflection in the train doors assures me I am exactly the woman I think I am. A backpacker gets on and pulls a map from the series of pockets on his pack. He notices me staring and moves closer to an older couple with beige luggage stacked in front of them.

A girl sitting near me who cares deeply says into her phone, "It's not like I really care." She wears a cinnamon-colored wig.

The man from the couple returns my gaze with an almost-smile, which cheers me.

"Uh-uhn," says the girl in the cinnamon-colored wig.

A child leans against her window frame, glaring at the passing train. A bowling pin surrounded by jags of neon that signify a strike. A man delivers a plate of food to a table.

The girl in the cinnamon wig: "How are you going to tell me who I am? Then when I call you on it, you've got nothing to say."

The flank of an overpass shines like abalone. The wig, the shine, the warmth of the metro's heat, like buoys bobbing on the sea of night. Listen. I am moving toward something, even if anyone watching would say I am only going back and forth on the train. I no longer want to keep myself hidden from myself.

It's Saturday, technically. Technically means that in every way that matters—emotionally, mentally—it's Friday, but technically, it's Saturday, the day I will be married. When I return to my room at the Inn, the Post-it on the lamp reads, DON'T FORGET TO GET MARRIED, the groom's back moves sweetly in sleep, and I think my head will explode but instead the phone rings and it is Rose, who is still my best friend. It's time to leave for the salon. Everyone is eating flagels and waiting for me, the hesitating beauty. Do I go? In this moment it is as simple as not wanting to disappoint a lobby of people with whom I share varying degrees of intimacy, some obligatory, some merely sketched out, some rich and entangled. There is no blanket of explanation that could cover them all. Do I go?

Why did I ever quit smoking, my grandmother said. *One of life's joys.*

I button a new shirt over my bare chest and walk through the antechamber into the hallway. The elevator brings me down to the lobby, where everyone applauds.

We take two cars to the salon, passing a bakery, a post office, two stoplights. The town is famous for its lake, bagel hybrids, and how little time it takes to drive through. The air is so cold I fear we'll crack as we run on tiptoes into the hair salon. My mother and my friends, their bodies swelled beyond childhood. Their C-section scars, their fractured attention spans. We were intertwined in college but no longer know who is sick or lonely or scared, as we shake out the cold in the vestibule. The receptionist announces who will go to which chair. I am the last assigned, so I watch my friends retreat to their stations where they explain the weaknesses of their hair, what years of abuse have done to it, ways in which it used to be lovelier. Requesting heat and products that tame.

I remember the way Simone said the word *experiment* and the client who fell through improperly laid insulation and now doesn't understand the idea of a folder. If you can get through your own wedding without an existential breakdown, I'm happy for you.

I follow the hairdresser to a station by the window and take my seat. I explain where I'm damaged. "Do your best," I say.

On the morning of my wedding at an early and incorrect hour that makes good people appear menacing the hairdresser says I am the calmest bride she's ever done.

"How do you be a bride?" I say. "This is the first time I've been one."

Most brides, she says, are filled with words and energy. A few moments later she adds, "Opinions."

The room is wide with flaking paint and so cold we summon breath. She winds my hair around an iron and cheers for a chugging coffee maker. She apologizes for the chill, the coffee's delay. I can hear but not see my friends, sitting on peeling stools and radiators improvised for chairs among stacks of boxes. The coffee maker mutters, a soothing sound. I leave another message for the reception planner.

"A wedding should exist in its own world," the hairdresser says. "Undisturbed by the petty crap that goes on in ours."

"That hasn't been my experience," I say.

Her lips are colored a shade of red that's meant to be fun, yet her downturned mouth creates the tributaries of some sad river that deepens her forehead. She's copying me; the tendency humans have to mirror another's pain.

"You're so calm," she says, thinking I haven't heard.

"I'm calm like a bird is calm."

"Ugh," she says. "Birds."

"Why does everyone hate them?" I say, continuing an earlier thought.

She says she once watched a seagull wrench a sandwich from a woman's fist. The woman held on. Tug-o'-war. "Eventually she gave up, the woman. The bird flew off with the sandwich."

I tell her that I once saw a woman mail her shoes. I don't mean in a package. She walked up to a mailbox, leaned against it for support while with a free hand took off one shoe then the other. She opened the box's door and slid them in, listened to them flack against the metal bottom, checked that they were gone the way you do a letter, and walked away, barefoot.

The story stops the hairdresser's talking, the desired effect, so I am free to consult the window and think of birds. I want to see a woman in a flattering trench coat hunched against the cold. I want to see a winter animal. But the day insists on parking lot and this corner of dumpster. Except for a car slugging by carrying its own weather system, the window never varies its point of view. Most people think you need shoes but that woman thought she was fine without them. I'm thinking, trauma is an elevator. A portal, I mean. An Internet.

The day requires me to get married. From another part of the house where she has been pinned and ironed, Rose arrives to say she is excited. Am I excited?

The salon has found its heat. Those who can, shuck sweaters to reveal short sleeves.

"Yes," I say.

She is the third friend to scoot around boxes to ask me this question. I've answered yes each time, but a particular tilt of the head makes it clear I've answered incorrectly. As the others did, Rose ticks through supplementary questions (*How excited?*) or makes a statement she believes is innocuous (*I'd be excited, too, if I were about to marry the greatest man on Long Island*), then leaves, shelving her confusion.

My phone buzzes on the counter. The tables came in, the reception planner says, the linens the correct shade of neutral. We are unaccustomed to talking to each other because I preferred to leave bridal opinions to my mother and mother-in-law. "Will you please add one person to table nine," I say.

"One person," she says in a way that means, *At the last minute?*

"Simone," I say. "A dear friend."

I hear the rustling of aggravation as she hums, fusses. "Simone . . . ?"

"Then it's set," I say. "I'm grateful."

"Who is Simone?" says Antonia, who has crept behind me during the call.

"A friend."

Antonia asks if I'm excited and I say yes.

I sit at that vanity for years, my mother and friends orbiting, offering barrettes, bronzers, taking them away, asking if the coffee's burned, convincing my shoulders down, discussing where they hold stress, Mother fretting over the carpet, referencing their lower backs, offering me a bite of whatever they're eating, fingertipping a eucalyptus mask over the apples of my cheeks taking care to avoid the vulnerable under-eye area, placing a phone to my ear so I can hear a questioning voice, taking it away, halving a flagel and offering it to me, someone at the door, a mistake, a new delivery, crumbs on my shoulder, this heel or that, this bracelet's sheen, these stockings have silk in them you can tell, a matter on the other side of the Inn, delicate empty boxes, Mother in new makeup, new Mother, bellboy at the door, something blue and something old (my heart) unable to rise to the occasion (my heart), a forgotten idea winks outside my periphery, can't catch it, mutterings on the edge of my hearing, don't tell her, tell her, a bouquet of laughter (my heart) tossed over the carpet, dropped, mother-in-law fretting on the other end of the phone, matter settled, matter unrelated, updated eyelashes, the desire to crawl into one of these boxes and draw vellum over me, with a damp washcloth whisk the mask away, show her the flowers, look at them, look at me, rise, heart, please, these are good people, rise before they see you in the mirror, such a beautiful. Girl, don't you think? Is that James with more flagels? Flowers hold stress in their stamens. Couches hold stress in their cushions. Barrettes gather hair. Gather the gathering items back into the boxes, offers retreating over the carpet, rejected jewels rewind into their cases, but there is one more commemoration—from a profound box, the hairdresser reveals *the veil*. Everyone is wild over this dash of lace on pearlized combs that possesses such gravity it pulls all the women from their chairs. All week everyone has been treating me like I am eggshell and the veil is the graduation of that feeling. I have become. So fragile it could be soiled by breath yet the veil persists across the room. Antonia won't hand it over. I'm not ready to stop touching it, she says. Center the breathless ecru comb at the nape. As the hairdresser presses it against my scalp, they unfold the veil out from underneath itself, look at her eyelashes against it, the rose rising on her dark skin, the scallop flush along my collarbones, black hair against the bone-colored everything, the most correct earrings, eyes in another place no matter, mind in another place no matter, the woman removing her shoes and lifting the door to the mailbox isn't worried, the bodies of my friends surround me, switch places, smooth the crinoline, what a morning, the sun is here ancestors be praised, couldn't have wanted, couldn't have wished for, I'm not ready to have this feeling, this feeling is not finished halving me, the veil is buckled hard against my scalp, such a beautiful. A finished bride brown in the mirror. Lined in striking pencil, articulated in ebony and red.

Antonia holds up a mirror so I can see myself from every angle. I cannot be mistaken for anyone else. The hairdresser gives a low whistle of approval. "She's the calmest bride."

Several moments pass, perhaps a century, until everyone is called by voices deeper inside the salon to their beautifying processes and I turn into a feather and collapse onto the salon seat maybe I am still there now.

A LOT OF PEOPLE LIVE
IN SANTA CRUZ

I've never made good money but enough to cover pride, so I pay for everyone's procedures and walk to my car. The car hisses as I bounce in place convincing warmth into my arms and legs. I drive in silence, lit cigarette balanced on my lower lip.

The concierge calls hello across the lobby. Hello, I holler, and point to my wrist where there is no watch. She shrugs as if to say, *There is never enough time*.

Other than my event-worthy hair and veil, I wear jeans and a button-down and carry nothing. A bride that stops at the neck. No attendants. I press the elevator's button and can sense the concierge debating whether to call out again. Her sincere smile, her hand hovering in the air. The elevator arrives. *Simone at the wedding*. The elevator lifts but when we three—myself, the elevator, my thoughts—reach my floor, the doors do not open. I've come to welcome these elevator delays, guilt-free moments.

I watch myself in the mirrored walls, veiled, slide down to sit on the floor and dial the reception planner. "Checking to make sure you've arranged a place card and seat for Simone."

"Yes," she says. "I've put her with the table you've labeled 'one-offs.'"

"Perfect." I hang up.

The doors slide open. The concierge's voice trails me out of the elevator. "I've heard it's good luck to say a rosary on the morning of your wedding. I have one at my desk if you . . ."

Minutes down the tree-lined road, the groom is being mimosa-toasted in his aunt Henshaw's home. The cake is in the shape of the lake. In the morning we'll return to the city.

Alone in the room, I switch the channel to a newscast and slide under the folded coverlet. From the shelf of sleep, I hear local news stories. Henrietta has opened a store during an unfriendly economic climate. Despite everyone's predictions, she is doing well. In global news, in towns around the world, people prepare for different holidays amid varied architecture.

The ringing phone wakes me. My armpits are damp, my leg cramped. Many minutes have passed. Possibly enough to comprise a substantial unit of time. Is it strange to take a nap on the morning of your wedding? A move that might land you on one of the lists the bridesmaids have spent the previous six months sending me: "10 Wedding Mistakes You're Unknowingly Making," "8 Horrendous Brides," "7 Trapdoors to Sentient Soul Disrepair," "4 Damaging Untruths."

"Checking in," my sister says on the other end, faux cheerful. "Are we ourselves today?"

"Everyone keeps congratulating me and asking if I'm excited."

I hear a cigarette being lit. "I read an article last week about a father who married his daughter. She beat out the sister, who also wanted to marry him. Congratulations, folks! You're in jail."

I wipe my underarms with a damp cloth and check my eyes

in the mirror. "What do you register for when you marry your father?"

"Birth control?" she says.

"Literally everything around me is white. The veil, the comforter. It's like I'm in an egg."

Simone doesn't laugh. "What are you going to do?"

"I don't know."

"Well, hey." I hear an exhale of smoke. "Take your time."

"Are you coming?" I say.

"No, dear."

I hang up and slide out from the covers, immediately cold. I've printed out Internet instructions on how to apply smoky eye makeup. My first attempt looks like bruising. I wash it off with soap and a rough towel and try again. The results are not perfect but better. A knock on the door and Rose enters, holding a glass of red wine. She sits on the toilet and watches me brush color onto my cheeks.

"I took a nap before you came," I say. "Is that strange?"

A look of concern passes over her face, but her tone is cheerful. "Anything you do on the morning of your wedding is natural."

We pass the wine back and forth. She lights a cigarette, reads messages of congratulations sent by friends who couldn't attend.

I curl the eyelashes over my left eye and listen. A friend from my past, a flickering almost boyfriend, has left a message.

I ask where he's living and she says California. She googles *Santa Cruz* and holds out a picture on her phone. Beach and evergreen. A crescent of low-slung houses and shining driveways.

"Don't we know someone else who lives there?" I say, and she says, "A lot of people live in Santa Cruz."

In the main room, Rose pulls open the closet and pales. "This is the wrong dress. This isn't the one you bought when I was with you."

I check. "It's the right one. I didn't like the other so I bought a new one."

"What was wrong with the first one?"

"Nothing," I say. "It wasn't my style."

She swallows an intended remark. This is what friends do, decide not to unravel you.

I undress until I wear only underwear and my grandmother's locket. I lift my arms and Rose slips the dress over my head. "How would you describe the Internet?" I say. "If you had to?"

She yanks the crinoline underneath the short skirt then massages the eyelet scalloping. "I wouldn't."

"Come on," I say. "Pretend you met a caveman who'd never heard of the Internet. How would you describe it?"

She lines my heels on the carpet and says she'd ask her stepfather.

"What would he say?"

"Put your shoes on." She kneels so I can lean on her and step into one heel then the other. "He'd say why are you worried about the Internet on your wedding day?" Heeled, I sit on the bed. Rose's mouth is arranged in the horror of concentration as she reaffirms the veil's combs pressed against my scalp. She's checking my moorings and riggings, as she has since high school.

"He is practical," I say at the same time she says, "He is an idiot."

Rose stands behind me as I evaluate myself in the kitchenette's long mirror. "Beautiful," she decides. "Let's take a selfie."

We smile at ourselves and count to three.

"There's a ghost behind us," she says, checking the picture. In the mirror the flash has imagined a human form.

"A trick of light," I say.

The phone rings. We jump.

"Who is Simone?" my mother says, calling from a room on the other side of the Inn that sounds like it is filled with aggressive classical music. Though we'd been maintaining a flimsy truce since I got engaged, I'd asked the concierge to put my room as far away from hers as possible.

"A dear friend," I say.

"It's too late to add someone."

"Mother, why do you sound strange? Are you unwell?" I tap my fingers. Rose mouths, *What's up?*

"Why do you keep asking that?" she says. "Worry about yourself. And whoever Simone is."

"A dear friend, I said," I say.

"I thought we were finished with the readjusting."

"I don't know what that means, Mother. Rose is here. She says hello."

My mother dons her public voice. "Hello, Rose." She reminds me only a few minutes remain before everyone is due to meet in the lobby then hangs up.

"If I asked you to lock my mother in a closet for the rest of the day, would you do it?"

"Is this one of your friendship tests?" Rose says. "I would."

"If I asked you to pull the car up and drive me away from here, would you?"

She considers then rejects concern. "I would," she says. "There's a late movie at the Sunshine. I was sorry to miss it."

I ask if it is *Beginners*, the movie with the talking dog who is optimistic about romance and I tell her I've already seen it.

"Too bad," she says. "Guess you'll have to get married."

She must leave to get ready. "Who is Simone?" she says. "You keep mentioning her. What we love, we mention." She hugs me and walks to the door. Her curled hair makes a pleasing shape against her shoulder blades that work in tandem underneath her sweater.

"Then I must love you because I mention you all the time."

Something about her small bones chugging against the thin sweater works up in me what I can only call a realization of the obvious: The floor we're standing on is the ceiling of the room below. And the floor of that room is the ceiling of another's. There's been recent renovation, which always creates friction. We trust so many strangers to build things that won't shatter. My heels dig into the flimsy synthetic that separates me from disaster. If Rose leaves I will plunge through the floor in an explosion of dust and debris, to the room below that, and below that, until I hit wherever bottom is. My knees will pop like kernels over heat. There is only a moment before everything explodes.

As I normally do when finding myself on the brink of something I don't understand, I ask an unanswerable question: "What's going to happen to me?"

Her eyes gain a faraway cast, as if she's seeing my future on the dense curtains that suffocate this antechamber, this room before a room. She thinks I am asking her to step-by-step me through the day. "You'll go downstairs, join the bridal party, and we'll go to the church where you'll get married. We'll dance and eat steak. We'll try to avoid your mother. You'll endure a few aggravating traditions. You'll go on your honeymoon and start your life. Like a million other women have done before you."

"A million," I say.

"A billion," she says.

"No honeymoon," I remind her.

"I thought you were going to stay out here, for a day or—"

"He doesn't want to miss work."

"Regardless," she says. "Like a trillion other women."

"If I told you my grandmother visited me in the form of a bird, what would you say?"

The concern returns. "You're scared of happiness," she says. "Consider the dress. Your old one was perfect yet you convinced yourself it wasn't so you got a new one you didn't need. You don't want to fill out the place cards so you invent a story about toothpaste. Or your grandmother. Or a bird. You don't want to meet the florist so you have a panic attack. You're scared to get married because you don't think you deserve marriage because you don't think you deserve happiness. You do. No matter what you've been through. When you find the right dress, stop looking."

She tells me my groom is handsome with non-thinning hair. His job can support the weight of two people, or more, should we decide to have children. Rose trusts this answer.

"It'll be over before you know it," she says.

"That's what people say about surgery."

At the doorway, she pauses. "What's all the stuff about the Internet?"

I borrow her unaffectedness. "Skip it."

Rose closes the door so it doesn't slam. For a moment I love her the way I did when we still wore crochet half tops, our brilliant skin hanging over cinched denim waists. To her, my hesitation can be discarded as jitters, a disturbance that people can explain and so allow. Only, it's not the question I mean, so her answer belongs to another bride in another room who really is wondering what is going to happen to her and imagines that whatever it is might be good.

That winter in New York was so cold people had begun to fist-fight on the train. Every morning the papers reported a new brawl. I'd seen one the week before, two women dressed in office casual, circling like predatory animals, rattling purses. They snatched at each other and fell into a thick slump of coats. Strangers pulled them apart, still hissing intimately. It had been cold for so long you couldn't remember how to feel at ease. My neck was always stiff because I slept shrimp-curled to contain heat.

People want to hear that foreboding zippered down my back but except for the fistfights, it was a normal Sunday. I was twenty-three, sleeping with a married man, just graduated from state university, and still living in the borough with my mother. I still thought I had a brother named Tom who was still in the city struggling to produce his plays.

I was standing on the platform when the R was taken out of service due to the city's new inclement-weather plan. I'd never heard of a train being taken out of service because it was cold. My plan was to borrow my grandmother's car to get to my barista job. The sky was blue. The parakeets were on the power line.

In the 1970s, a cargo ship unloading in the navy yard dropped a crate that cracked against the concrete and exploded into thousands of parakeets. Meant for Argentina, they were accidental immigrants. Unlike the common budgie preferred by phantom grandmothers, these birds had indigo foreheads, startling blue tail feathers, silvery throats. Every time I saw one as a child was a holiday. I was always pointing them out, to myself, to family, to strangers. Searched for them constellated in the branches. Spread out over the sky in improbable arcs. I giggled alone in my bed thinking of their velvety bellies and read everything possible about them. Parakeets can swivel their heads 360 degrees. They are frightened of whatever is above or behind them. They are passive-aggressive, anxious birds, but tenacious. They figured out a way to stick in New York's endless gray calendar, building their complicated, multi-unit apartment colonies over the spires and trees of my grandmother's neighborhood. Mobilizing out of the fog. They signaled other, non-shitty, warmer lands. How many died trying to fly back? Did they ever escape the DNA echo of desire for the bone-deep heat? Did they ever stop wondering, what is this imagination-less palette, this cold like a grudge?

The mean trick of trauma is that like a play it has no past tense. It is always happening.

My grandmother is always opening a box of gingersnaps when I am always arriving.

"Perfect timing," she is always saying.

Like the parakeets, she is an accidental immigrant. Her mother was banished for becoming pregnant with her. Stinking of cows from her muddy mountain town, she carried my grand-mother with her on the boat. To come here, the land of above-ground trains and five for a dollar.

"For what?" My grandmother cracks a gingersnap in half and chucks the small side.

I am always eating from the pile of discards that collects by her elbow. "So I could get a good job making coffee."

"How about you make me some coffee," she says.

I use the silver percolator, tamp the ground beans into the up-per chamber, taking care none of the silt slips. My grandmother lifts a pair of binoculars to her eyes. "What's she doing?" she says about a neighbor. "Hanging clothes in the cold?" She sits, miser-able. "Lilian died."

"Rec center Lilian?" I backhand crumbs into the trash.

"She's the third one from the old gang," she says. "I have to buy dresses to take my mind off it. Death is expensive." The grounds swell. I tip the coffee into her cup and add a cube of sugar. She tries it. Nods.

"Worth it?" I say.

"Nah." She hands me the keys. She wears two sweaters under a robe and refuses to buy a winter coat. Everything in her nature prefers hot. She is a parakeet.

In the middle of the harbor another immigrant stands in her ox-idized dress. I walk to the car under the gaze of several small birds.

When I get to work the writer is already drunk at a table telling Yuna what he thinks about this writing stuff.

Yuna stands on her tiptoes to change the radio's channel to a cooking show she likes. The host's campfire voice makes her want to spend her day off cooking even though she's terrible at it. We've spent whole shifts discussing a meal she's ruined. I like how she remains baffled by her mistakes. I'm already looking forward to hearing the unexpected way she will botch the macarons she plans to try that weekend.

"You could braise beef in milk, I suppose," the host says.

"Rose hip," Yuna says, "and vanilla."

A man enters. He is average size and wearing a dark coat over dark pants. Yuna plans her grocery list. I plan to return my grandmother's car. I still have use of both legs. A man enters and hovers in the doorway's misleading sunlight. Maybe he shivers, the divot between his eyes too deep, or the grimace on his face telltale. But no one notices when the man enters. On him hangs the rest of the afternoon and our lives. He favors his left leg so that shoe's sole is slanted. A slanted man enters when we still have plans and, after pausing in the doorway, moves toward the counter, allowing the door to shut behind him. The events of his life have brought him into the path of everyone in this coffee shop. Ours, ditto. A man enters like so many men only this one contains a particular curdle. He has already pivoted away from some important principle, has already professed online the things he will do. He believes that immigrants are soiling his bright country. I don't notice him consult his pocket, the way we check whatever's wrong with us, patting it, making certain it's active and dangerous. I froth milk behind the counter, listening to the writer talk about beginnings.

"'Once upon a time' is a terrible way to begin a story," he says. "It's inexact and trite and a lie. Much more honest to begin a story with 'This never happened.'"

Another man's voice on the speaker wonders aloud to his guest about roasts. "How does a classic roast differ from a Yankee pot roast?"

"In a Yankee pot roast," his guest replies, "you'd add the vegetables as you go so by the time the roast is cooked, the vegetables are tender."

"Tender," I say to Yuna, who winks.

The writer says there is nothing being done in modern fiction that is what he would call new. He has been short-listed for a prestigious prize won by a woman whose father works at a famous magazine.

"Nabokov built homes for his readers," he says. "Every chapter a room."

"This is definitely not new. You sing this song every day," I say, and Yuna agrees.

The writer's cheeks plum. I ask the man who has entered if he has decided what he wants. He shakes his head no.

I say, "Let me know if you have any questions."

The front door opens and a couple laughs in. Their movement jostles the man who has already entered.

"Excuse me," they say.

"Yes, in the coq au vin," the cooking show guest says. "Absolutely in the coq au vin."

"I'll sing this song until someone hears me," the writer says. He is white and working class. I find his cynicism harmless and entertaining during a dull shift.

"When you cover a pot, it's going to boil and that sort of rolls the vegetables around and they fragment, become fragrant."

I bang the silver jug on the counter to create more froth. "I want your life," I say to the writer. "Drunk at noon. Espousing your bullshit theories to baristas."

"It's a hard life," says the writer. "I don't have health insurance so I can't even go to the hospital and complain."

"Raise your hand if you have health insurance," I say to Yuna, the couple, the writer, the man.

The couple lean against the counter, deciding on a flavor of ice cream. We're almost out of turkey, a fact I've told Yuna twice. The man reaches into his pocket. A small bird lands on a tree outside the window by the writer's head.

"Look," I say. "A parakeet."

"A parakeet?" the writer says. "A fucking parakeet?"

The man pulls the gun from his pocket, raises it shoulder-high, and fires into the shape the couple make against the counter. The girl slumps into the display case. Time leaves as the silver urn falls to the floor and hot milk splashes against my calves.

"How do you get the crispness?"

"A heavy sear on the outside."

"What about using guar gum as a thickening agent?"

"I stick to the traditional."

The man fires again at the woman he has already hit. Her boyfriend turns as if he will reason with the bullet that pushes him back into the display case. The glass splinters. I can't remember what I'm supposed to do, I am behind time. Yuna is underneath the counter then I am underneath the counter. I reach for the phone but don't know how to use it. Which buttons do I press? Yuna grabs it and dials. I hear her jagged breath, smell charred wood.

The squeak of an overturned chair. Scuffling, and there is another shot. A short, smothered yelp. The writer.

I hear the unmistakable whine of the bathroom door. Another shot.

"Do you have special pots that you use for braising?"

"Dutch ovens are the best. But you can braise in anything."

"Anything?"

"Anything. Well, not anything."

"Come out," the man says.

"Is he?" Yuna shakes. "Talking. To us?"

"What happens with the leftover braising liquid?"

"You certainly shouldn't throw it away."

The man vaults the counter. The full menace of his body is between us. The sound of breaking glass. He drops the gun and Yuna kicks it toward the windows. He scrambles for it. A whimpering that could be human or machine compels the room. We scrabble like crabs. Something explodes near my ear. Yuna is still.

"Use it in risotto?"

"That's a good idea."

The man realizes the silverware tray is next to his head, reaches in, and produces a knife in a time that seems impossibly brief.

"No," I say, as if the moment hovers between happening and not and I can kick it toward the latter by refusing consent.

He brings it down into my thigh, retracts it, and brings it down again. It works. Over and over, he brings it down. I want to tell him that the knife doesn't go there. He has already hit more times than I can count. One must imagine it brings him relief. I am still responding as if in a normal human situation because pain has not yet arrived so I think maybe there is time to reverse these actions.

This is what they call trauma logic, which is indistinguishable from dream logic.

Violence like snowfall dulls sound.

Blood leaves me. I'm still reconciling this man with the milk and the parakeet and the writer and the machine's shining wands and my grandmother and the car and the train and the cold. I am still five minutes before, when no one has been shot. Splintering glass and new screaming doesn't hinder his work on my leg. Time gulps, rewinds. I note the room's bodies in a part of my brain that is as far away as childhood. A new figure ascends at the end of the counter. Sound returns. A long, colorless scream. I yearn for the internal darkness that beckons and intoxicates me. The figure at the counter raises something above itself and the walls of the room retract. A holdout in my thigh relents—after, I'll hear it's my deep femoral artery. The retracted walls move forward and the man's neck kinks at a troubling angle. He abandons his work, his hand rests on my pulverized side, the knife slides down our bodies balletically, the way a leaf falls onto a lake. He is skin-thick with psoriasis and has a history of pulling his wife through the local bar by her ponytail. I'll know this later when I stare at the report for days, before I relearn how to walk.

Fear arrives late as usual, filling everything. Yuna rasps politely, gazing without focus toward the ceiling. I want to say her name but my throat won't work. I have only a sense of where she attends school and for what, but I like sharing shifts with her because of the cooking thing and because she doesn't chatter for the sake of noise like other baristas. She, the man, and I lie in milk and blood. I reach for her. I say her name. I think if I can touch her, I can heal her. God? I ask. I ask, Please? God.

"Grilling will be coming up, when we get away from this snow."

"It's hard to believe we will ever be rid of this snow."

"Let's get back to fennel."

"Let's."

"Do you enjoy fennel?"

"Fennel was the first vegetable I ever braised."

"Really?"

"Yeah."

I ONCE SAW A WOMAN
MAIL HER SHOES

In one of the unexpected events that arise in emergency—I am left alone in the ambulance, covered in a thin blanket, breathing into an oxygen bag. I'm stable and conscious so not the priority. Inside the coffee shop, a team of paramedics work on Yuna. Through the ambulance's back windows, I watch police cars block the street. Cloudless. My grandmother will be watching the second of two episodes of her favorite game show.

On the perpendicular road it is a regular day. There, oblivious to our crisis, a woman halts in front of a mailbox. Leaning on it for support, she removes one shoe then the other and picks them up, two plastic fish. She pulls down the mailbox door and slides the shoes in. It is not possible I hear them flack against the metal bottom yet I do. She peers inside, closes and opens the slot until satisfied they're gone, the way you would check on a letter. She turns and walks away barefoot on the frozen pavement.

An EMT climbs into the ambulance to double-check my

vitals. "Yuna?" I say. She presses her palm against my heart for a few deep breaths then climbs back out to join the others.

At first, I am an injury novice. Months of ice chips, shuddering to the ground after physical therapy. Eventually, a step, another. My gait is different post-injury, like someone who no longer trusts the ground.

Invisible injuries that are harder to articulate level me. My married boyfriend disappears. Friends abandon me after I breach some unknown time limit of healing. Rose says I imagined the woman who mailed her shoes. It is the first of many times my perspective is doubted because a man decided to delete a shop of people and rendered me unreliable. I stay inside then retreat further. I trim reactions, halt passion before it blossoms into something that can wreck me or, worse, disappoint others. After a while, I doubt my own perspective. Previous injuries are triggered. Snubs, insults, the times my mother ignored me. Reinjury is worse than injury. I don't know which to manage first.

People who want to be supportive say the gunman was an animal but animals have reasons to kill. They want to eat, they want their family to eat. They don't destroy their habitat because they're frustrated. People who want to be supportive say it wasn't personal, but what that man did to me was as intimate as a lover. To be hurt so intensely that one can no longer feel the weather.

I spend years in this emergency state until I am an injury veteran.

In the hospital I become known for conversation because I don't judge and harbor suspicion for anything a large group believes, like religion and insurance. Many patients were failed by both. I talk to everyone in the hospital. Nurses, priests, visiting family members, patients with far more frightening injuries.

One afternoon, a visiting lawyer asks if I want to join his law firm in a new position: biographer. Juries are so desensitized by mass violence, he explains, that savvy lawyers must deduce new ways to tell a story. What do I know about reptiles?

One day, my grandmother calls to ask what the Internet is. I lie and say it's a phase. The next morning, she climbs to the top of a ladder and falls. I sit with her for a month, trying to will her out of a coma, as approaching death carves her. I play her favorite Lawrence Welk records. She prefers to stay asleep. My mother shuts down the machines. They tell us it can take moments, a day, or a week. That we'll sense death is imminent when she stops urinating. On day four she opens her eyes and sucks in a choking breath. Death enters. Her chest rises then is still.

I no longer feel collected and I am no longer afraid of death. I've played its records. I ask my grandmother, haunt me, please. Like god, she fails to appear.

Who does appear is an elementary school principal with no apparent hang-ups who sings songs to children. On our fifth date I prepare a symmetrical meal. I cut my pork breast into logical slices as he asks for my attention.

"This is the time," he says, "that I am going to ask you to marry me."

He doesn't second-guess my perspective and he has never given me an orgasm. He will never lie to me and he will never make me howl with laughter. He says commitment is as simple as yes or no.

"Okay," I say. We finish our meal and call our parents. Everyone is thrilled. The decision brings me closer to a societal norm. For the first time, my mother sounds like she recognizes me. *Oh. You're a human girl.* Sports television before bed. The reliable click of the remote. For once, trouble at bay. Age recedes into its deep chamber. I assure myself that no one marries for love anymore. If lust ultimately defroths into friendship, I'm ten steps ahead. A human girl, making rational decisions. The next morning, wedding plans begin.

A WEDDING IS AN INTERNET WHERE EVERYONE SEARCHES FOR THEMSELVES

I gather only what I need into a pearl clutch and am careful to close the hotel room door as quietly as Rose did even though I'm almost positive there's no one left inside. Waiting for the elevator, I search the Internet for *bride in space and time*.

A scene from *Fiddler on the Roof*, backlit bride on a bare stage. Disaffected bride and groom at the back of a bus, the last shot of the movie *The Graduate*. Bride chained to a desk, urinating in her dress. Bride holding bouquet, floating downriver. Bride on wide lawn. Frowning bride in regalia. Dead Renaissance bride mourned by man wearing cassock. A 1950s bride winking, smoking. Bride holding gun, eyes caked in mascara. Bride wearing jockstrap. Pastel bride flying over town holding chicken. Bride with beard of bees.

"They all look sad," someone says, and I realize I'm speaking aloud in the elevator that jolts to a halt. I've grown fond of the Inn's idiosyncrasies. I assume this is a particular type of elevator that breaks on the way to every destination. Who can't relate? I consult the lit panel and the doors, firmly shut. I call the front desk.

"Will only be a moment," the concierge says.

A text comes in from the groom: *I can't wait to marry you.* Pressure builds in my throat. "No rush," I say.

"I'll bet no rush." She laughs as if I've made a joke. "You've got nowhere to be."

In the mirrored walls, refractions of brides avoid my stare. I step in and out of my ecru heels. The dress's hem rubs against my bare legs.

The hanging syrup-colored orb is a camera. I wave. The concierge must see me, alone in an elevator wearing a wedding dress and veil. The sulfurous scent of the stopped elevator deepens. I smell my pulse where a few moments before I'd swiped vetiver.

Her voice comes through the box: "Are you excited?"

The elevator depresses its brakes and brings me the rest of the way down.

"It's fixed!" I step into the lobby, noting a distinct disappointment in my chest.

Rose and the party have been waiting long enough for their faces to rest into expressions of anguish. My mother searches a mirrored compact as if trying to locate a criminal. Our limo idles outside. Everyone turns their rouged, matted, highlighted complexions to me and applauds. Strangers sitting on an opposite couch follow the party's gaze to where it meets me. I blanch under the attention.

"We've been waiting for the bride," Aunt Henshaw says. "We've been eating those bagel things and talking."

"Flagels," Antonia says.

Someone has contoured my mother. "My god," I say. "You're commercial-pretty."

"I've been blowing my nose all morning. I swear there's a cat in here." Her gaze scans me. "That's the wrong dress." Her tone is egg whites whipped to stiff peaks. "That's not the one you bought."

"It's the other dress I bought."

"What was wrong with the first dress?" she says.

"Too fussy."

"I think this one's perfect," Rose says.

"What have you been doing all morning?" my mother says. "I called and called."

"I was in the lobby, Mother. Telling everyone how excited I am."

"How excited are you?" Antonia wants to know, and I tell her there is no mechanism on earth that can measure an amount that large.

"What about the scales that weigh an elephant?" the groom's nephew Rodrigo says, sitting on the arm of a couch. I've never seen him sit in an actual seat. He is a quiet boy who only pipes in when he's thought of a sarcastic comment. "What about the scales that weigh a jetliner?"

When I talk to Rodrigo I make every statement a question, reflecting the brattiness I divine in him. "What I'm talking about isn't necessarily a solid?" I say. "So the examples you're using don't apply? An emotion isn't a jetliner? It would be like weighing the sea?"

On the pocket-size screen of his video game, Rodrigo's avatar sprints through an expanse of fog-lit mountains. In real life the kid is blond and scrawny. In the game he has chosen a dark boy with muscles. "He" rolls neatly under a barrage of gunfire, then completes an unlikely jump to tag a yellow disk triggering the mountains to part. He makes a dismissive sound and returns to his game where "he" levitates through a cavern of candelabras. I didn't want to invite Rodrigo, or any children, but the groom insisted.

We file outside where the air is a crisp threat. I am seated in

the limo when a thought launches me back out, jockeying everyone between me and the door, which is everyone, because as the
bride I was allowed to enter first.

In the lobby, the concierge has retreated behind the desk and
is tapping at her computer's keyboard. She looks surprised to see
me. "Can I help?"

Whatever reason I've returned has been torn clean out. Nothing in the room reminds me. The untidy fire. The smell of cheap
cranberry candle. The twenty-dollar bill in my hand.

"Did you forget something?" she says.

I hold out the bill. "A tip!" I slide it over to her.

"Too much," she says.

"For your daughter, then."

"No." She slides it back.

It is odd behavior to run back to tip when you're a bride. Everyone seems to be thinking it: the strangers, the fire, her re-
sumed rapping on the keyboard.

I return to the limo and the driver shifts us into movement.
We ease down the driveway to the main road. There are only five
stoplights until the church. I counted the day before.

The trees are furred with thick needles that insulate against
what the lake can throw. It is midday on a regular Saturday for
everyone else. A mother hurries her children along the sidewalk. A line at the bakery. A group of college-age students sit on
a low wall, exchanging a mug of something hot. The limo passes
through town like a cloud over the sun, reminding passersby of
an opulent event, whether they want one or had one or hate the
idea. Every time I see a limo, I think: tuxedoed teenagers.

We pull beside a man tapping his fingers against a steering
wheel. A girl on the sidewalk insists to her mother, cheeks wet
with tears.

After five stoplights, the limo reaches the church.

We're early. The guests are still arriving. The bridesmaids call out the names of people they recognize as we hide in the car.

Finally, all the guests have climbed the steps and vanished behind the heavy doors.

Someone says, "It's time."

We disembark from the limo. An official countenance settles over the party, silencing the bridesmaids who let me pass like a specter from one world to the next.

The driver leans against the car, hands folded against her thigh. Even my mannerless mother recedes as I push through the oak door to the vestibule where my stepfather stands, staring at a collection of pamphlets shoved into wall cubbies. My mother insisted he'd walk me down the aisle. I fold my hand into his elbow's crook. The bridesmaids file into the antechamber, ducking out of view from the open middle doors. Organ music pumps through the church.

My stepfather's mahogany musk hangs in the air along with incense from an interior room beyond the vestibule. I clasp the unfriendly fabric of his rented tuxedo. Someone tucks my hair behind my ear. Someone gently wrenches my purse out from under my arm. Someone shows me where she keeps her mints in case I want one later. Someone says, "Any minute now." The groomsmen line up like soldiers. Whispers of guests make angelic noise that chorus around the chancel, my mother asks the usher, *What's the holdup?* A missalette rockets to the ground followed by nervous chuckling. Someone apologizes for the wait. The priest was in the bathroom. Every church wedding throughout history has begun late on account of a priest being in the bathroom.

Rose said it would be over before I knew it. Which is what I tell my clients about suffering. Time spent away from a lover, a plane ride. Everything in my battered life has led me to this vestibule, this hyphen of space that will join my life to another's. The man tapping his fingers on the steering wheel. The girl insisting to her mother. I would have traded places with any of them. Is this correct? Maybe all brides feel this way but are sworn by oath not to tell.

Aunt Henshaw loses then finds her pashmina. "It's like when you're looking for something, you find it," she tells Antonia.

"So true," Antonia says.

Someone says, "It's time."

The organ music switches from meandering to focused, as if it will deliver us down the aisle with its certainty. My mother marches through the middle doors on the arm of a groomsman. One by one, each woman vanishes into that sacred slot until only my stepfather and I remain.

"Where are they going?" I ask him.

"Where are who going?"

I check his watch, two fifteen. "No one left but us chickens," I say.

Someone says, "It's time."

Occasion steals my memory. I can't remember what hairdo or which veil I chose.

"Am I wearing a tiara?" I ask my stepfather.

Confusion uglies his face. "Are you wearing a tiara?"

We pose in the center of the doorframe. Several empty pews away, the guests pivot to see us.

The music shifts into the furtive and holy song the groom and I chose the month before. It made sense then, but now I can't re member why we wanted such a militaristic dirge as my stepfather and I glide through the standing guests. Here is Rose's stepfather, festively belted. Here is a cousin, petrified in rouge. Here is Rodrigo, stiff with occasion. I thought I could count on him to stick out his gross tongue, but even he realizes that what I'm entering means no fun.

I do not remember my stepfather's grip or having to recalibrate my steps to match his. One step, another. I dismiss the thought that no one has said I look beautiful. But as the groom's sleeve comes into view, promising the rest of him on my advance, this bothers me. I'm not a woman who trades on beauty but you're supposed to tell a bride she's beautiful even when she's not.

Granny, I miss you. There are all these people on earth who aren't you.

The groom comes into full view. A cracked map of blood vessels reddens his nose and cheeks. He's been drinking already. The girl insisting to her mother on the street was speaking to me. The groom sees me and grins. Beside him, four groomsmen are arranged by fondness. We reach the altar. My stepfather kisses me dryly on the cheek and takes his place in the pew, noticeably relieved. I face the groom.

The priest ahems and asks if we have come here of our own volition. Yes, we say, and this signals the guests to be seated.

The priest says some love is deep but unfulfilling, a durable towel on a rack. Some love is general, a sense of community, a garden that is watered from within. Love can be a hummingbird that lands on a jut of wood and, finding it undesirable, flutters off to try another.

A guest in the front pew moans erotically. The people around her titter.

"We are right to exult over these kinds of love," the priest says. "But they are not the reason we stand in this room today."

The love that gathers us is more reliable than some stupid bird, more durable than your pitiable towel, it doesn't need your dumb-ass water, but contains the kinetic energy of dynamite or a car crash. The kind of love that is not like but is a bridge.

Bridge is *bride* with a *g*, I think. Then: Bride has a bird in it. Has anyone else noticed? The groom is not the type to think of things like *bridge* is *bride* with a *g*. He is no doubt thinking about love forming itself into pillars and counterbalanced pulleys, laying itself down over a choppy sea.

I want to lower myself onto my stomach and place my cheek on the thick carpet. I'd like to nap. I'll address the congregation: If it's copacetic, I'll die until this is over and you're gone. I don't need a pillow or any attention at all. Don't touch or speak to me. Please continue without me. To debride means to remove damaged tissue from a wound. If I take myself away from this ritual, everyone will heal.

Bridges are built to sway in bad weather. How did engineers figure that out? Left to myself, I'd build one with no flexibility and it would snap under the weight of the first car. And everyone would wonder how I could have made such a mistake. But I'd wonder why anyone trusted me to build a bridge in the first place.

Rose's face makes it clear that mine is not performing correctly.

I should not be thinking of bridges but the priest doesn't seem to be talking to me. I will have thousands upon thousands of days and this is merely one of them. This thought brings relief. My shoulders loosen. My breath deepens. I gaze at the giant colored windows and over the friends in the pews who will catch me in real and sanctifying hugs as soon as I am free.

The priest tells me he is going to list a bunch of obligations and I should notarize each one with my voice.

As he speaks my locket falls open. My grandmother stares unimpressed at the groom from her half heart nestled in my collarbone.

I am filled with longing so rich it has mass and cuts me. It is composed of the people who are not here. My prickly, unkind grandmother. Who only once pulled me into an approximation of a hug, so awkward we both laughed. My sister.

The best man pulls a ring from his breast pocket and hands it to the priest. He's been married twice yet still his hand quivers. His new girlfriend sits in the second pew weeping, loving him. The priest holds the ring above his head. The attention of everyone in the church turns upward to a nine-hundred-dollar one-carat diamond. The priest says the ring is a symbol of our love.

"I don't like diamonds," I'd told the groom when we picked it out. He said, "Everyone likes diamonds."

The groom slides it onto my finger.

The priest pronounces us married.

Everyone cheers. The bridesmaids press tissues against the corners of their eyes, any one of them willing to trade places with me. They've said as much, at the bachelorette party and the shower. Two of them immediately fantasize about other men when their husbands go down on them. Possibly they fantasize about the groom. I apply this to him and evaluate him anew. He takes my hand and holds it, shoulder-high. He pumps his other fist in a cheer. This is wild and unlike him. We flex and jerk through the hooting crowd to the back of the church where we pivot to re-greet the people we've just abandoned, ready to receive them. The organ celebrates as we verso recto, greet and re-greet.

What a service. What a day.

"Traumatic brain injury and PTSD," I tell a guest who has asked about my job. "Normally during on-the-job accidents."

"Sounds tough."

"It is," I assure them.

Three of the groom's college friends stand at the side of the church, whispering while wearing smiles. "Is her brother going to be here I hear they're not talking still they're restaging that play of his the one that caused the damage but won him the pull him here Pulitzer? Her brother? Tron. Who? Tom. Does she have any? Family? What was it he had this weekend, a show? Pulitzer be here the play that won is causing all the pull him here."

They assume their words are private yet I hear them because of the architectural voodoo of churches.

"Let them," I say to the pink-sweatered cousin who has always bothered me because she is identical to my second-grade teacher.

"Sorry, dear?"

I say, "Traumatic brain injury."

"Like football players," she says. "How sad."

My mother ushers the cousin toward the door. "No one wants to hear sad things today."

The final person greeted, we join the rest outside. The limo driver chucks her cigarette into the street. The groom and I dance down the steps, through the people we've abandoned then received, and abandon them again, stepping into the limo with the rest of the groomsmen and bridesmaids. Rodrigo wants to ride in the limo again but the ride back to the Inn will involve drinking and adult talk. I like watching as he's carried weeping to his mother's car.

Someone says, "It's time to celebrate."

We drive back to the Inn. Five stoplights.

Combined for the first time, the bridal party reaches full power. The girls arrange their dresses and fix their makeup. The grooms-men avert their eyes. Their partners are waiting in parking lot traffic but that doesn't mean they can't flirt, does it? It is taking longer to get back to the Inn. Five stoplights. We've already passed this intersection, haven't we? The window is obscured by a groomsman's vest as he makes a point about America's justice system. Trade winds, I think. Time difference. "How long have we been in this car?" I say. "It's supposed to be easy to drive through this town." A groomsman shrugs. "A couple minutes?" Someone lowers a window. "You got somewhere to be (waiting for this moment, a moth double-axles in, considers Rose's hairdo then a display of purses, flirts across necks and shoulders, lands on Antonia's bracelet before diving up between the women, a quick swab of the upholstery, the ceiling then the seat, the ceiling then the seat, Antonia's shoulder then the seat, then, certain, question-marks bluntly to where I sit next to the opposite window that I lower so it can cartwheel into the air that dusk ((Dusk? It's too early for dusk.)) has charmed. The moth's trajectory from one side of the limo to the other takes seconds and no one notices except me), wifey?" the groom says. Champagne pours itself. An argument blooms at the front of the limo about a court case being tried in California. Two sides advance. The case is about a Hollywood producer who has been accused of rape. Why is anyone talking about anything other than the wedding or us or the idea of the wedding or us? Weddings are mirrors in which everyone sees themselves. People query it for anything that applies to them then return to their lives. An Internet search: Me. How their hair compares in the reflection of other people's milestones. Does that mean this wedding is an Internet? Also, wifey? Dusk dips into the swells made from mountains and trees. Wifey? What other tendencies will be unlocked because of this serious paperwork?

Judging by the week's events, the moth is my grandmother. Or, a future checking in on me. I am not misremembering that it takes a hundred times as long to return to the Inn and by the time we do the sky is pitch-gray.

The limo screeches to a halt.

"Why is it nighttime at four in the afternoon?" I say.

Everyone screams, "We're here!"

There is a wedding in each of the Inn's two banquet halls and the other bridal party has already arrived. They fill the lobby's couches and chairs with their dresses, suits, and accoutrements. Another bouquet and photographer. Another bride. Another groom. Another frigid afternoon.

The other bride leans against a pillar, an attendant bustling her train.

"Fight, fight, fight," whisper-goad our groomsmen.

A sign directs our bridal party to the correct banquet hall.

The members of the other bridal party smile as I walk by. In the presence of options, the mind leaps to compare. Rose assures me I am prettier. But I like the other bride's wide, kind eyes, her eating-disorder hair. She does not wave but emotes toward me as she gets tied tighter into her dress.

Simone is not in the lobby, or on the flight of stairs, or in the hall's side room, where our guests hold abbreviated plates of food and sip cocktails. Seeing us, they use their free hands to applaud soundlessly against their wrists. Someone hands me a plate with shrimp and bacon.

After the groom is taken away by coworkers, I discard my plate and walk to an elevator in a brief and empty corridor. I press the button for down, pulling the silken body of a cigarette from the dress's infrastructure. The doors open and I press the button for the lobby. After a few moments, the doors reopen with a ding-ing sound and I step out, imagining the pleasant burn of nicotine against my tongue. But I am again in the cocktail room. The elevator has taken me exactly nowhere. I retreat into the glowing box and stab the lobby button. The doors close. A stomach jump of movement. Dinging open, the same scene is revealed, cordials being exchanged over hors d'oeuvres.

James pushes a cart of ramekins by. "Everything okay, ma'am?"

"Everything's great, James!" The doors close. The stomach lift of movement, thank god, the ding.

The doors open onto the same scene. I experience a sensation of having blown up a balloon too fast. Every elevator in this build-ing is a Borgesian nightmare. My mother there-she-ises through the nonspace that connects the cocktail party to the elevator ves-tibule. She appears pin-lit, always asking a sympathetic audience if they can even believe me.

She uses my elbow to steer me into the arms of Aunt and Uncle Henshaw.

"You're married!" they say.

Behind them, dressed in green, Simone lifts a glass to toast me. The sight of her heavy-lidded gaze, demure sweater dangling from her forearm, brings me to tears. I excuse myself and walk over.

"Are you in there?" she says.

"I am. Are you?"

"Not sure. Ask me something only I would know," she says.

"How much do you want to murder Mom right now?"

"Her taupe stockings are enough to make me flee. But I'm here."

"You are." I try to hide a tear but she sees, waits for me to compose myself. "How was it?"

"I can't remember. You're sitting with the one-offs," I say. "The groom's college friends."

"Grabby, athletic types, I imagine."

"Only when they're sober."

Waiters in formidable button-downs escort the guests to a bigger room with round tables. The groom and I sit at what's called a sweetheart table. Just he and I.

We eat steak in lobster sauce and have a choice of three desserts. I watch Simone on the other side of the room make polite conversation.

"You look happy," the groom says.

The wedding cake arrives on a rolling table, containing ingredients you can't even taste.

My mother informs us that we must greet each table as a couple. She knows the groom's tendency to join any clump of unfit men discussing the game, and my tendency to wander. "It's etiquette," she says. "Them's the rules, spring rolls." She uses old-timey slang when uncomfortable. A droplet of gravy clings to her cheekbone where she has applied bronzer. The tenor of her voice makes the gravy quiver.

Table nine is as good a place as any to begin: the bipartisan remnant bag of friends and colleagues. Among others, it includes Coleen with one *l*, Colleen with two *l*'s, LaShonda and her girlfriend, and Simone.

"You look beautiful," Simone says.

Everyone pauses over their desserts to say congrats. The groom makes a joke about a cabinet at work, which isn't funny, however because of the benevolence of weddings, the table erupts into laughter.

Simone gazes serenely at the groom. Someone asks what the groom thinks about the late slide that ended a beloved shortstop's season. This cannot be discussed from a seated position, yelling over centerpieces. They pull him into a suited huddle.

"The bride would like a cigarette," I tell Simone. "What do you think is the fastest way to get outside?"

She points to a door on my left. "I'll join you."

I fit a cigarette between my lips and hear the whooping that the groom reserves for male friends. It's a sound that gets stronger as it proceeds, that simultaneously divides and singes, that prompts the world's insecure girls to stay in the classroom instead of joining the others for recess, that reaches a silly bend near its middle, so that a few guests glance over.

The door leads to a salmon-colored hallway. To our right hangs a portrait of the Inn's proprietor, a ruffled older woman. To the left, her equally ruffled husband. Nameplates pose beneath their chests.

Simone reads. "Estelle and George Paradigm."

The hall is long and smells like chicken soup, not the expensive kind with garden-thick carrots, but the canned kind you buy when obliterated by fever. The jovial cigarette bounces, fastened to my lip by saliva. I slide my hands along the smooth walls. I lunge to see how deep I can go.

"You're having fun," Simone says.

"You're here," I say. "What changed your mind?"

She looks down the hall, pivots, looks the other way. "You'd do it for me."

Under the skirt's satin exoskeleton are eight sighing layers of crinoline. In this quiet space I hear them whisper. There is an interior and exterior zipper. Double-zipped into my wedding day. No bride can handle this shit herself, the skirt reasons, demanding attendants or mothers. A decade has passed since the night Ada and the husband stared at me in disgust. I've already put it up for sale on the same website, using the original listing's photographs. A buyer messaged me immediately, a woman who lives in my neighborhood and uses a criminal amount of exclamation points. She will be the third bride to wear the dress.

"I'm going to leave soon," Simone says. "Seeing Mom has put me in a bad mood."

"I understand."

At the end of the hallway, where we expect a door we find a turn that leads to another run of hallway. I silly-walk down that one, too. Simone trots on her perfect heels. We reach what we assume will be a door but find another curve where two paintings hang.

"It can't be," Simone says. "The Paradigms again? Hey," she says. "This is a . . ." She circles the figures with her hands dramatically. ". . . false paradigm."

I light a cigarette and she takes a drag. "How did you find this place?"

"On one of our trips to see his family," I say. "We signed the contract and then they renovated so we felt like we got a new building for a good price."

The weakness of this logic seems to depress her. "This building has been renovated?" she says. "To look like the hotel from *The Shining*?"

"Long Island," I say.

"Estelle dear, your taste sucks." She blows smoke at Estelle's image.

I take the cigarette back. "I look forward to seeing your rendering of my wedding onstage."

"Cheap shot."

Passing the cigarette back and forth we reach—it cannot be—another hall. In front of us, as far as I can see, is indistinguishable from where we came from, a salmon-colored future.

Simone says, "Is this the longest fucking hallway on earth?" at the same time I say, "We're trapped."

I debate going back. No hallway is endless. But this one is doing a good impression. I take a deep drag. "You won't, will you? Use this?"

"It's a story. I can't always know. Like what you do?"

"Help injured people tell their stories in court to get them money so they can afford medication?" I use the cigarette to "point" at the jury, the client, the medication, the idea of justice.

"When you put it that way it is very different," she admits. "Still. You understand the sociological impulse."

I hand her the cigarette. "I understand that you strip-mined the worst day of my life."

She exhales an angry plume of smoke. "You keep saying—"

"Because you haven't acknowledged."

A loud ding startles us both. A series of clicks. An overhead sprinkler activates, sending water against us and the walls. Simone's dress is speckled with wet. "Run."

We argue as we jog down the corridor away from the twitching sprinkler, cigarette bobbing on my lip, chased by the sound of my hushing skirt, around a bend, where we halt. A hallway double the length of the others combined stretches before us, so long the end appears blurred.

"Don't yell at me because you married a normsie."

We run, no longer talking. The skirt whispers faster. HUSH-HUSHHUSHHUSH. I'm only half aware that the cigarette is ash-ing into the drape at my neck that Ada's listing described as a *décolletage dream*.

A cry builds in my throat. If there is no door at the end of this hallway, I will scream.

Another turn, and we finally reach a vestibule with a door leading outside flanked by two more portraits. George and Estelle again.

I push through anticipating outside air but we end up in the reception room, groom still huddled in a corner with his work co-horts, fork poised over cake, listening to LaShonda. Mother and stepfather across the room. The smell of coffee and raspberry. Flickering votives because they were cheaper than candelabras. After-dinner music has begun. The bridesmaids conga around the floor. Again I've tried to leave the reception and failed.

"Something is happening." I heave like I've been held under-water. "I can't leave."

Simone's voice betrays concern. "Are we having identical breakdowns?"

But then there's the groom's aunt Grace! Suddenly batting around my neck! Can she see what's inside my locket? I show her—grandmother on one side, empty on the other. She calls a few others over. Everyone wants to touch my dress and hair.

"Simone," I say through gritted, smiling teeth.

"Ladies," Simone says. "Would anyone like to see the tattoo I got to commemorate my transition?"

The ladies turn to her, rapt with attention.

"Go," she says.

I walk with purpose through the guests. People part, assuming as the bride I have urgent business, but what business could I have? Like the President of the United States, my personal effects have been removed and are being stored elsewhere. They've only allowed me a compact mirror and a tiny comb. Simone is right. I am having a breakdown. My grandmother has come to me as a bird. I've inhabited my mother. My brother returning to my life as a woman is the only thing that makes sense.

In the bathroom, toiletries preen in baskets. I spray deodorant to see the mist. I unroll a stick of gum into my mouth, then another. I decide to see how many I can fit into my mouth. If I can fit the whole pack, everything will be okay. On the sixth something catches in my throat and I choke. On the seventh I pause, wait for nausea to clear. On the eighth, a pep talk. The ninth won't make it in. I spittoon the gum into a toilet. The challenge has blurred my lipstick, but someone who owns a lot of baskets has thought of that. I have my pick of shades, choose a dark one, and take a long time making my lips perfect.

I gather the skirt and climb onto the toilet. Tonight, these people will drive to their homes on desolate highways. Tomorrow these people will not be wearing these clothes or eating slices of shoddily conceptualized cake. They will not be thinking of me or this wedding, so I will be free from obligation. In a day they will return to their jobs and I to mine. This event will move into the realm of that which is mentioned occasionally. Later, if I happen to say that I felt like a photocopy of myself, membrane-y, barely able to understand how I got here, perhaps time will enhance their ability to empathize. If I can be patient. But that doesn't help me, balanced on a toilet in a bathroom stall. The room swishes its hips. Light bulbs dim and buzz. Everything rights itself for a moment during which I doubt my perception. It happens again. The room switches sides with itself. The bride is certain. Overtaken,

I fall through space and time. My forehead hits the stall door and the momentum easily breaks the flimsy lock.

Every time I'm offered something with almond, the same promise: You won't even taste it. It shares this with coconut, another ingredient recommended by its inability to make a goddamned difference. Why not just stop using both? I know people like this. Recommended by their inability to influence. But they are dependable, they fill out the party and are more liked than I, subtle as anchovy. Jesus Christ, what are we all doing?

The floor rushes forth like a hard hug. Sometimes I mistake presence for fondness. Even though those who are absent are normally the ones I love most. Perhaps because so many in my life have said, "I'm here, aren't I?" when I've asked to feel their love.

She came to in a red booth, forehead pressed against a lino-leum table flecked with mustard-colored sparkles.

Behind her, the sound of a throat being cleared, as if its owner sensed himself being overlooked. A reptile wearing a suit and tie squinted into the glare of a laptop. The room contained two rows of identical booths, each outfitted with a personal juke-box. She used the side dial to flip through music choices. Every song was Jerry Lee Lewis's "Great Balls of Fire."

Copper lamps hung above a wide counter. Beyond the counter, a swinging door. She sensed a stillness on the other side. Empty shelves and an oven. Except for the reptile's claws tip-ling against his keyboard, there was no sound in the diner. No staff. She could not see out the fogged windows but knew it was evening. On the other side of the counter, a bank of coffee ma-chines made her stomach growl. Coffee could correct a series of wrongs inside her. The reptile did not look up from his screen.

"It's serve yourself." He flicked his eyes toward a shelf of mugs nearby.

She crossed behind the counter and stood in front of the mugs. Each was emblazoned with the name of a state or country, as if collected in gift shops across the world. She chose Spain and pulled the plastic lever, releasing a stream of fragrant coffee. She stirred sugar into the coffee, tried it. Too strong. She added more sugar, poured creamer in and watched the liquid turn beige.

The reptile felt her shadow over him and glared as if she were the sun.

"Do you mind?" she said. "Normally I like being alone but it's been a strange week."

"You are the bride?" he said.

"Spooky. How did you know?"

"You're wearing a wedding dress." He slid a pile of newspapers away from the tabletop, as if to make her comfortable, which didn't match the character she had built on his scowling face and lack of eye contact. She sat across from him, blowing on her coffee.

"Do you mind if I ask," she said, "where we are?"

"Not at all." He appeared to weigh different tacks. "In a manner of speaking, we are in a diner at the end of the world. But in another manner of speaking, we're also not. There are many, many worlds, and many diners at the end of each one."

This sounded reasonable. She wanted to ask which world but worried it was a stupid question. She chided herself for being intimidated by a reptile. She couldn't be expected to know everything. He had to expect questions. She sipped her coffee and focused on his laptop. "Are you working on a novel?"

He laughed. "I'm a daysleeper. I run a Japanese lifestyle blog," he said. "Tokyo is thirteen or fourteen hours ahead of America's East Coast, depending on daylight savings time. When it's evening here, it's day there, so I sleep during the day and set my alarm for

7:00 p.m., to wake up when their market opens. I blog tips and advice for the day's trading, with culture and fashion thrown in."

"You're a vampire," she said.

"So are you, it appears." His tone was pleasant. She had really gotten him wrong.

"How often do people ask you for tips?" she said.

He braced, in anticipation of her asking for a tip.

"I have no money," she assured him.

"I wouldn't be able to help, anyway," he said. "I deal mostly in futures. Guessing how valuable commodities will be. If people will want rice or gold next year as much as they wanted it this year."

"You're a gamb—"

"I'm not a gambler." He caught her comment on its rise. "People who think of the market as a gamble don't understand it."

"I don't understand the market," she said. "I can't even explain the Internet."

He shrugs. "The Internet is a tapestry that covers the entire world. Billions of people hold its edges. It's similar to the market." He pretended to hold a cloth in his hand. "When one person in Australia goes like this "—he "lifted" the fabric then "lowered" it to its original height—"the people in Sweden feel the ripple effect in the market. When someone goes like this over here"—he "yanked" the fabric back—"the people over here feel it. With everyone lifting and yanking, the area in the middle is a sea of waves and flat places and movements and is constantly shifting. And then there are rumors. You hear that people holding the fabric over there are about to drop it. So you want to drop your side. But then they don't drop it, and then other people you hadn't anticipated drop theirs. Others pick it up. It is ever changing and impossible to predict. Gambling implies that there is rhyme or reason and those who are able to count fast enough can figure it out. The truth is, the market is influenced by forces impossible to chart. It's like fashion. It never ends."

"The Internet is nature," she said. "Wind that doesn't begin or end."

He jerked his chin to the counter, the windows etched in condensation. "There is nothing you can think of that the Internet is not."

"Are we the Internet?" she said.

His laptop emitted a sound like a tiny wave crashing. A familiar voice broadcast from an overhead speaker. "We're working on it. You'll be down in a jiffy."

The diner tilted to one side. Nausea lurched in her stomach. The diner tilted back, righted itself, but the ground no longer felt solid. She touched her cheek and felt indentations made from the plastic booth, chevron stripes.

"Is this a ship?" she said.

He blinked several times but did not answer. The crashing-wave sounds increased in volume.

"Friend," she said. "Am I awake?"

A scorpion hissed from the bottom of her cup. She hurled it into the aisle. The overhead voice assured her that James was on his way.

"There's been a mid-session rally," the reptile said. "Stay calm."

The fog crept higher on the windows. The reptile pressed a button on the jukebox and Jerry Lee Lewis sang. She widened her eyes to clear her suddenly misty vision. Sound of foghorn. Sound of bells. She balled her fists and swiped at her eyes and opened them again. The music emanated from within a miles-long expanse of fog, tuned by distance that continued to grow. When will

James get here? she wondered. Everything will be okay once he arrives.

She stared backward from a force that was pulling her away no matter how she struggled. "I can't leave before James gets here."

"We haven't reached our lowest numbers," he said from the end of a long tunnel. "Your grandmother says even though we've gotten off the floor, we can always go lower."

"How do you know my grandmother?" I say, cruel reality waking me.

"*You're fine,*" he said. "*So kind . . . I'm gonna tell this world that you're mine, mine, mine, mine.*"

W*ake up*, my grandmother says.

I regain consciousness in the Inn's bathroom, a little girl I don't recognize standing over me, tiny hands clamped on my shoulders. She asks if I'm all right.

I struggle to steady one leg under me then the next. I reassemble in front of the mirror as she gapes. My forehead bears a red welt where the floor slapped me. I riffle through the basket for makeup.

She asks where all the gum went. "The pack was full a minute ago," she says.

"I ate it. I'm the bride."

"There's another bride here," she says.

"I'm one of the brides. Are you the other bride's flower girl?"

She nods.

"Are you having fun dancing?"

"I was," she says. "But then they asked everyone to come onto the dance floor for a couples dance so my cousin and I were dancing and they said anyone who wasn't married had to leave. And then anyone who was only married for a day. Then, anyone who was only married for a year. Until only my old aunt and uncle were dancing, and everyone cheered."

"People who don't stay married get shamed," I say.

She nods. "You really like gum, huh?"

"Sure do."

"Your dress is pretty," she says, exhibiting an undetected sweetness that makes me regret eating all the gum. "Do you like it?"

"What a thoughtful question," I say. We examine it in the mirror. "I like how it fits my waist."

We wash and dry our hands. I follow her into the other banquet hall. As she walks, she reties the bow making a pleasant horizon on the back of her silk dress. Her arms are too short and can't reach. The bow ends up sagging. I'd help but you don't touch other people's children.

The other bride sits on a chair in the center of the dance floor, howling with pleasure as the bridesmaids circle her. The deejay plays a popular song and the other groom beats time on his leg amid a crescent of observers.

The bridesmaids file away to make room for the men who've been called to the floor for the garter toss. One of them wags her finger at the groomsmen to say, *Be good.* The men stand with their hands folded, waiting for their part. The little girl stands to the side, shuffling in time to the music.

I've seen dozens of garter tosses and they always produce the same sensation of hollow ritual, cheap lace slid up a stranger's thigh to tantalize. I return to the banquet hall that applies to me.

The bridesmaids and I used to make yearly excursions to Atlantic City. On this past trip, bachelorette themed, we stayed a few nights in a casino. Our rooms overlooked the poker tables. We spent three days hungover eating cheap eggs and breakfast meat. Outlet shopping and the beach. Periodic interruptions by husbands and children on the phone. Long after my friends fell asleep every night I watched the dealers dole out chips and cards. Give then clear. When to stick and when to fold. I watched them until I was so tired it looked like they were dealing pearlized eggs, clearing glitter-gates into shimmering decks.

The bridesmaids are girls from high school who were surprised when I asked them to fill important wedding roles. They don't wear lip gloss anymore. More than half of them had ill-advised marriages in their early twenties out of which they quickly ejected.

On this last trip, everyone secured their belongings into their car trunks by noon on Sunday, apologizing out of the parking lot in reverse. After they left I dragged my suitcase onto the beach and ate a breakfast taco and watched the ocean throw itself around. Pigeon colored. Exhausted and flat, but honest. I thought about second marriages, what my friends call the real ones. They defend indefensible aspects of their slovenly, lucky husbands and stay in yearslong ruts because they cannot fathom two failed marriages. What's wrong with divorce? Concluding that staying in the thing would be more illness than salve, snipping and cinching it, freeing one to pivot from what is not working and grow stronger in a different direction. If a plant insists on sending energy to its dead flowers, it dies, but it only takes itself down. Humans are not plants; they cannot keep rot to themselves. How dead marriages seep into the soil, dulling everything around them.

A marriage that furnished love and was relieved of its misery at the appropriate time so its participants could go on to love again, isn't that more of a success?

I sat on that beach after all my friends had gone home and

locked eyes with a scuttling seagull. Too intense to be mistaken, I was definitely its subject. We stared at each other until I knew it would be me and this seagull forever, and then do you know what that gorgeous, thrilling, winged heartbreaker, who I'd only just given my love to, had the gall to do?

The bridesmaids circle me, chanting my name while I do every dance move I can think of.

Across the room, sitting amid abandoned chairs, a man watches us. He wears formal trousers and a tuxedo shirt scissored down the middle. Blood leaks from a cut on his chest. Tom.

SARA SOMETHING

The last time I saw my brother was in an upstate mountain town at his wedding to a girl named Sara Something who I'd caught in no fewer than four lies in the time she dated him:

1. The time she lied about letting his cat out and Oberon was missing for three days.
2. The time she said she was going home after the birthday party and I saw pictures of her on social media out at bars.
3. Every time she said she was clean.
4. Every time she said my brother was clean.

That was when Tom was doing everything half-heartedly. Dating her, writing, he was even a half-hearted drug user, which turned out to be enough to get him hooked. He told himself this story: He could marry her and if not be happy, belong.

On the morning of their wedding, I watch Sara cross the mountain retreat's lawn from my second-floor room where I drag an iron over my dress. Her veil bobby-pinned aggressively around her gel-slicked topknot, she appears disturbed, wearing only a slip. The camp is arranged in a friendly L-shape around a lawn on which the invitation encouraged us to bonfire, sing, or "just be." The day before I'd watched Sara Something's cousins suck through cigarettes at the picnic tables, a pile of discarded ends hilled by their ankles. Now it supports a phalanx of folding chairs pointed toward an arbor accented with fake flowers.

Though the area is experiencing a heat wave, I wear a sarong to cover my scarring. I'm the only member of our family present. Everyone else has given up on Tom, who didn't visit me in the hospital or help with our grandmother's funeral. The decision to attend his wedding came after realizing the geometry of immovable emotion: I'd regret going and not going, equally. No one clings to a brother like a little sister.

From above I watch Sara Something bang on an adjacent room's door with an open fist. Adrian answers, bare-chested, wearing a towel. He must have arrived during the night. He shuts the door with her inside.

On the cabin television's lone channel, fly fishermen stand in a river casting golden lines so thin at certain angles they disappear.

Sara Something emerges from Adrian's room and tears across the lawn. When she reaches the arbor, she yanks one of the flowers out and resticks it farther down. I agree with the new placement.

She jogs the rest of the way to her room and vanishes inside. I hang the dress in the closet as the phone by my bedside rings.

It's her. "There's a problem," she says.

In one of his spectacular displays of poor decision-making, Tom has gone clean. That morning Sara found him puking into the toilet in the cabin they rented for the week.

Sara has fury's logic. "He considers it a wedding gift. It's one thing to go clean and another to do it when you have to be suited and reasonable within hours for cocktails. We're supposed to toast our parents, for Chrissake."

Tom is in withdrawal and has flushed his stash. Sara Something has decided: someone must find heroin for the groom. She asked one of her cousins she thought might be holding but he's clean, too. She sounds astounded, as if the world has conspired to chemically unplug in an effort to screw her wedding day.

"Did he think about how stupid it was to go off the day before our wedding?" she says.

"I wouldn't know about that." I wonder why she called.

"My cousin says there's a suburb near the city where we can get what he needs. I can't go, obviously. They can't go because I can't risk my parents finding out. I'm being honest: they hate him."

Sara Something thinks the first-rate shit she says is justified if preceded by *I'm being honest.* One of the fly fishermen plunges into the banks of a churning river, casting his silken webs. I unmute the television to hear the river.

"I understand," I say. "I really do."

"They don't want their daughter to marry a junkie," she reasons.

"I believe that is the situation my brother was trying to help you avoid."

"Will you go with Adrian and get him help?"

"Can you please ask my brother to come to the phone?"

"He's throwing up in the bathroom. He's like, writhing around."

I hang up, dress, and secure a few items into a purse. On the lawn near the arbor, Adrian waits, wearing a button-down, jeans, and a blazer. We take his car. Muscles show up through his jeans and shirt. I'm in my younger stage of overfunctioning, so I natter on as he drives. I ask when he got in and he guesses, late. I ask how the drive was and he says, uneventful.

"I thought he was clean," I say, and he says, "I thought he was, too."

"Are we going to talk about this?" I say.

He grimaces sweetly, as if trying to clear a low ceiling. Being disappointed in Tom brings him physical pain. "If you'd like. I'd just as soon find his drugs and get back."

We follow the cousin's directions to a house in a manicured suburb. Greek columns accent the front porch.

"The Parthenon?" Adrian says, climbing out of the car.

We rap on the door and a visored woman answers, holding a baby who glares at us. It feels like an indictment.

"Sara _____ sent us," Adrian says.

The woman yells for Jessica, turns, and disappears into the house.

I ask Adrian what the name is that he said, and he says, that's Sara's last name, and I'm surprised because it is ethnic-sounding and she doesn't seem capable of anything interesting and then I forget the name wholly in the next moment when a younger woman in workout clothes emerges from a back room and bounds up to the door.

"You didn't invite them in, Elizabeth, oh my god." She ushers us into a gleaming kitchen under a barrage of salutations, apologies, explanations. The original woman, Elizabeth, and the judgmental baby sit at the table eating carrots from a mug. Jessica asks how Sara's cousin is and oh my god, how's Sara?

We say she's fine. In fact, she's getting married today.

"Amazing," Jessica says. "Whoever would have guessed that

Sara would get married. You remember Sara," she says to Elizabeth. "Sara." Her exuberance elongates the name to five syllables.

"Who?" The mother feeds the baby a spoonful.

"Sara-with-the-leg-braces Sara."

Elizabeth shrugs. "Sara," Jessica says.

"Have you been living here awhile?" I say.

"In this house? We don't live here." Jessica covers her mouth and giggles. "Can you imagine?" she asks Elizabeth, who pauses feeding the baby to laugh.

"What about leg braces?" I say.

"It was the worst," Jessica says, suddenly reverent. "She couldn't walk for like a hundred years."

The kitchen is lit from orbs sunk into the ceiling and appears to not contain dishes or glasses except for the carrot mug. Jessica says she doesn't do business in front of the baby and asks if we'd like to go to her room where there are snacks and chairs.

"Wait." I pull an envelope from my bag, slide my finger under the seal and wrench it open. Inside is a card with a picture of a brightly colored car, tin cans trailing its bumper. *Just Married!* Two bills fall out. "Use this," I say. "It's a hundred and fifty dollars. Is that enough?"

Jessica hits a pretty pose against the counter. "Totally."

Adrian leaves and I stay in the kitchen with the mother.

"Is that even your baby?" I say.

Confused, she looks at the baby as if he has made the remark. I hear the pulsing of music from the back.

"Right," she says, seemingly to no one. "That Sara. I just remembered. One of her legs was shorter than the other. So she had to use braces growing up. She had surgery in high school, I think. Straightened her out. She was always kind of a bitch. Did she get any nicer?"

I shake my head no. I should thank her for her hospitality, but out of some protest having to do with my brother and the position he's put me in, I don't.

"Cute," I say, about the baby.

She blinks. "You want to feed him?"

"Oh," I say. It's not an answer, but we both know I mean, no.

He fights the carrots. I've never seen a baby who actually wants to eat. On his bib, a tiny crab holds two mallets like castanets. *Fun time*, it reads. Is the crab excited to eat or be eaten? The baby is finished with the carrots and with her. He screams as if trying his voice out, collects himself, screams again. Elizabeth pages through a magazine of what looks like doghouses. This baby is schedule-less, it is easy to tell, and must react to the existential dread of life without a map from its mother. A schedule is a gift we give children so when they are adults they can deal with the anxiety of loss. I wonder if the baby will be the kind of adult who always has to be surrounded by people.

When I consider that once my brother was a baby wearing a bib it becomes painful to look at the baby.

"They're taking a while," I say. "I should check on them."

She gestures wordlessly toward the hallway. I follow the music to a room where Jessica and Adrian sit on a couch, touching knees. His hand is on her thigh. When I enter they look up as if emerging from a deep well.

"Wedding," I remind him.

He charms her down the hallway through the kitchen and front door.

"Sara. Say hi to that girl, okay? And congratulations on her wedding?" She phrases it like a question, which feels correct. She coos at Adrian, says to return when the next delivery comes, she'll have better shit then.

"No thank you, darling," he says. "I don't touch that stuff."

"Don't like to have fun, Adrian?" In one motion she purrs, pivots.

"I love fun." He gazes at her kindly, tone falling off a cliff. "I'm just not a fucking addict."

"Goodbye!" My voice is bright.

Adrian places the paper bag in the back seat of the car.

"Ouch," I say. "Rough on her at the end there."

"I don't like people like her," Adrian says. "Who take advantage of the vulnerable so they can rent mini-mansions built to look like coliseums."

"Crazy about Sara though, right? Leg braces."

"Not everyone is all one thing."

I ask if that means he likes Sara for my brother and he says that's not what he means. The highway is vivid in summer, oil slicks and rainbows. Queen Anne's lace frames the road as we drive. A day to read a book by a river.

"A hundred and fifty dollars is a nice present," Adrian says.

"That's etiquette," I say.

He presses on the accelerator.

I say, "I'd stick to the speed limit."

Sara Something is in her wedding dress when we get back. Asymmetrical, one-shoulder, bias cut, with fancy-cheap features like abalone buttons meant to wow. She takes the package into the bedroom. A few minutes later she emerges, followed by Tom.

"Hello," he says. "It's nice to see you. I'm getting married today." He holds his hand out for me to shake. A tremor pulses in his wrist, climbing his forearms into his shoulders. His panicked eyes swipe the room, and his mouth goes stroke-slack, losing to darkness.

"What kind of garbage shit did you get him?" Sara says.

I loosen his tie, unbutton his shirt. "We need to get him to the hospital."

"He can't go to the hospital." Sara Something is in shock. "We have to get married."

Adrian and I carry Tom in his wedding suit to the car. Adrian drives while in the back seat I try to keep my brother awake. He doesn't hear me screaming instructions. I call the hospital and when we arrive the doctors cut through his shirt. Pearl buttons arc out over the floor. They nick his chest with the scissors, slide him through the doors then through another pair of doors then another. Adrian and I stand in the emergency room, in shock. One of us should return to the mountain retreat and tell them the wedding's not going to happen. Adrian says he'll do it and I will stay with my brother. Jobs decided, he doesn't move. I reach out to steady him, worried that now that we are out of trouble he will keel onto the shining floor. But instead he says, "I keep wondering when the adults are going to show up."

"I think we're here."

When I'm allowed to see Tom an hour later, he is sheepish, charming. Relief dulls my anger. We both know that his hand, posed on the sheet a few inches away from his body, is an offering. I do not take it.

"You are a little shit," I say.

He agrees. "But please know it's only because I'm so deeply unhappy."

That is the last thing he says to me the last time I see him. The final time. Pale, in a torn dress shirt, attached by his wrists and heart to a bleating machine.

Sara Something sits on a couch in the hallway. "This was supposed to be a happy day." Her voice is soft. "He blames your mother for everything, you know. What could she have done that was so bad?" I'm surprised to find she is on the outside of my brother's confidences. This has two effects on me: proud of him that he still understands humans enough to know who not to trust, and sorry for her because I know how cold that ice is.

I want to escape to my car's warmth but I say, "My mother had kids because she thought she had to. Then my father died and she didn't know what to do with us. And she really liked quiet. Tom is not quiet."

We share a huff of breath, a half acknowledgment. Her eyes quiver with tears. "Your mother is awful."

"She's just a regular person," I say, stiff with loyalty. "Not everyone has the same kind of family." I leave her, baffled, in her fancy-cheap dress.

I buy vanilla wafers and a soda from the vending machine, admiring the macabre designer who put a player piano in the lobby. I sit in my parked car. "You're welcome, by the way," I say to no one.

My family has never been good at joy but in tragedy we excel. We're skilled at belittling an enemy to entertain a sick person. Birthdays, anniversaries, and other celebrations in which the point is to express delight find us thick and insecure. Not sure what to do with our hands or our reasonable comments that everyone seems to think are morose and irreverent. But if you need a date to a divorce filing, or a partner to choose the headstone . . . Happy people stand in rooms like balloons. It's enough to spark a panic attack. So we rebel and puncture the balloons, turning occasion into tragedy, at which we can then excel.

I wonder what it must be like to be so addicted to something you can't see it has incinerated the tissue that binds you to others. And then I reject this point of view, jettison the years spent wishing my devotion could make Tom capable of relation-ship. I'm relieved I will never have to see him or any of these people again.

How could I have known how incorrect the landscape of his body was? How could I have guessed that instead of dying, he'd write a play about my life?

I drink the soda and decide to make my home in other places, until what remains in the car is no longer sibling to anyone. The hospital doors slide back and forth, letting in the sick and the well. The sick and the well. The sick and the well. I've already spent a year healing in another hospital. That's all the time I'm willing to sacrifice. A doctor exits. A woman. A family. Over the hospital's roof, an unfair expanse of stars.

Here is my brother, the groom, in his shredded wedding shirt, years later, his irrepressible eyes, all the tousled, nervous parts of him, leaning against a pillar in my reception hall.

And here are his wedding guests, shimmering beside mine. The anisette of that upstate retreat mixes with the mason-jarred gardenias of this inn. Between my guests I glimpse Sara Something's mustached cousins. My brother's guests are dressed for outside, flip-flops and shorts. My guests are for cold weather. Stockinged, suited, coated. Them denimed, faded, hasty hair. Us pressed and dry-cleaned, tamped with pins and lotions. For a moment, the reality of the day shivers and welcomes all possibilities. Sara Something's mother accepts a mushroom cap from the groom's first boss.

The guests from my brother's failed heroin wedding will ask the guests from mine to dance. The polite staccato introduction to a minuet. Sara Something's aunt in a sundress veers through a line of partygoers, clasped to my stepfather. He bends her into a dip, her mouth open, gleeful.

That party then and this one, now. Two sets of invited guests. Close enough that the years of divorces, bad investments, marriages, and other betrayals glimmer and turn friendly, manageable, as if any struggle we've ever had with a loved one can collapse if the right song plays.

My brother beams at the dancing. But it is my sister, Simone, who leans in to whisper, "I'm sorry. I won't use your life again."

"I forgive you."

The guests from her wedding fade. Something in this room—me, I suppose—reality, returns to its rigid state.

"Is there anything you need?" a waiter says. Is he from that time or this? Is his question literal or figurative?

"Anything like what?" I say.

He gestures to the area below my left elbow.

I'm holding a giant knife, flanked by only my wedding guests who gape at me like I owe them violence. Vanilla almond with lemon basil. The groom looks as if he's watching me take too long to hurl myself above a lake on a rope swing. He yearns to follow. If only I'd jump!

"Cut," he says.

I puncture the top layer of fondant and bear down into the tiers. The flash of cameras and phones. Everyone loves cake so much they can't stop clapping.

My mother says, "Cut!"

The guests yell, "Cut!"

D own a hallway punctured by portraits I find another staircase. I climb ten flights before I realize the number of floors
doesn't match the exterior of this inn that has only five.

The navy carpet here is different from the floors beneath it.
I pass several unmarked doors until I find one that bears the sil-
houette of a woman. Inside, my mother-in-law sits on a chaise,
staring at a photo that at my entrance she slides into her purse.
I apologize for bothering her and she apologizes for needing a
breather.

I check myself in the mirror. "You don't have to explain."

"Thank you," she says. "It's a. Beautiful dress." She speaks
like she always does, in fits and starts, as if whatever she says has
only recently replaced a thought she liked more. "I was sitting
here thinking of New Mexico. The houses."

"I've never been," I say.

"The first time we went my husband assured me I'd hate it.
He said I wasn't built to withstand heat and the sauces would be

too spicy. I loved it. Loved even more that he was wrong. I ate every green chili I could find. He didn't know all of me. Even after so many. Years. When you first began dating my son," she says, "I didn't like it. You had no family. Only your mother. I couldn't understand. Where were they? Everyone has family. Christmas, birthdays, you never have anyone. And you never seemed to want anyone. It bothered me. But then my husband explained something and I never thought about it again."

She wants an encouraging remark to finish but I remain silent.

"What he explained was, you probably wished you had a family like ours. And then my heart opened to you."

The truth was, I never wanted to attend their family's gatherings because when I was with them I missed mine so much it set me back days. I longed for my elegant, skittish, fucked-up brother. My razor grandmother. Even my mother. And then I'd have to acknowledge that I was missing incorrect, anxious freaks, and that I was one of them. People with good families can't fathom those without. Or that we don't want to borrow theirs. It soothes her to think I envy her, so I don't correct her.

Instead, I say, "I do have family. My sister is here. She's here."

"I didn't know you had a sister!" she says.

"She's always traveling because she's so talented and successful."

"I'll meet her," she says.

"You will."

She moves to leave. "The last time I was in New Mexico I saw a dog sleeping in the back windshield of a car. As the car was driving! Inside the window, like . . ." She does the slant of the windshield with her hand, then makes the shape of the dog. "Right in there."

When she leaves one of the stalls opens and the other bride emerges. "Hello," she says, standing next to me in the mirror.

"Hello," I say. "I didn't know anyone else was in here."

We speak with the instant intimacy of women who are experiencing profound change simultaneously.

"Congratulations," I say, and she says, "You too."

I ask how her day has been and she says, "The baker misspelled my name on the cake. After I triple-checked. My husband says I'm making too much of a big deal about it. Still. Best day of my life." She smiles. "Husband!"

She says, "I love saying it," at the same time I say, "It's weird."

"You're allowed to make a big deal out of whatever you want," I say.

"That's what I said." She raises her eyebrow to me in the mirror. "My family hates the fact that he's older than me by fifteen years."

"Do you notice the age difference?"

"Nah." She replaces the lipstick cap. "Only. I don't want him to die before me. I couldn't bear being on this earth without him."

"That's a nice thing to say," I say.

"I'm a nice girl. You are, too."

"No," I say. "I'm a mean girl, tired of pretending I'm not."

She tells me we don't have to take the stairs because there's an elevator. I tell her that I've been having problems with them but she says trust her. We get in. Two brides in an elevator. One of them having the best day of her life. Ding! A pang of betrayal when the doors open at the lobby floor.

"Have you had any trouble with these elevators?" I say.

"The only trouble I've had is my name being spelled wrong on a cake. Which is really no trouble at all." She pretends to anoint me on my hands, cheeks, forehead. "Energy in you and on you and around you." She turns and walks to her reception hall. "Goodbye," she says. "Good luck."

In my absence, the Hollywood argument from the limo has reprised and escalated. Groomsmen Chris and Nigel are captains of the disagreement, each side believing the other possesses sociopathic hearts. Chris insists on a minor detail. Nigel believes no one experiences pain like he does. They shove each other. A chin grab. They scuffle on the ground. The groom laughs molar-wide as the bridesmaids pull the men apart. Blood grows on Nigel's temple. His wife dunks a linen napkin into a wineglass and applies it to his wound.

The underpaid, merciful deejay, who has no doubt witnessed a million embarrassments, plays an infectious dance song, summoning everyone back to jubilance. Everyone is satisfied the brawl is over. Everyone wants to eat dessert.

There is a tearing sound like someone is unzippering the world. The deejay removes her headphones. Simone and I, my mother, and the groom's family consult one another to find the source.

"What is that?" Nigel says.

"Stay still," his wife says.

We don't have time to investigate. The ground beneath my ivory heels lurches. Simone's knees wobble inelegantly over the churning floor as a crack appears beneath our heels. She and I wonder at it, a slow-moving but determined snake through the linoleum and concrete. It perforates the floor into segments that tremble and pitch. We watch the rupture fracture into other fractures, and others. If it's an earthquake, it's a remarkably specific one as it only disrupts where the bridal party stands. The lights over our section burn out with loud pops. On the other side of the room the deejay stares blankly toward us, some of the guests stare wide-eyed over paused forkfuls of cake as we lurch and pitch in the sudden dark. Steady and reliable is the turntable, but even it skips, and the Go-Go's, as insecure as anyone else, repeat their weak manifesto.

Simone and I cling to each other on the remaining panel. The groom, my mother, and my stepfather struggle on a shuddering piece. The yelping groomsmen yank their wives to safety.

We got the beat, the Go-Go's sing.

"Hold on," Simone says. The quaking produces a cavity I tumble into, vaguely aware of other bodies falling around me. Dust presses into my eyes and nostrils. My throat sputters. I choke and cough. The veil catches on jagged concrete and rips in half.

I mean to say *I knew it* out loud, but sound is deleted. I don't know whether I'm speaking or thinking as I fall. We land one floor below in an ungraceful heap of natural materials. Simone, my mother, the groom, my stepfather, two bridesmaids, and, like a dream, James, who rushed to help when he heard the yelps and swearing.

"Are you okay?" the concierge calls from above.

Simone pulls me to my feet to assess injury. "We're fine," she says, baffled. The groom helps the bridesmaids stand. Hip deep in insulation and debris, we look to the shocked faces of wedding guests peering down at us through the hole. My mother moans, rubs her ankle, and leans against my stepfather. We are disoriented but intact, having fallen into a storage area for what appears to be gigantic bales of cotton. Cirrus and cumulus.

"We landed," Simone says, "on clouds?"

"Next week's conference," James explains, pulling himself out of the wreckage. "How we can learn more about technology by studying clouds. Or vice versa."

My stepfather frowns at Simone and me. "What are they doing?"

Suspicion narrows our mother's eyes. "They're laughing."

Everyone wants to help. One of the groomsmen hooks his hands under Simone's armpits and lifts her out of the debris. She smooths her dress, still laughing. The groom attempts the same with me but loses his footing. He tries again, I aid him by jumping, but he can't get a grip. I half climb, am half lifted out, and sit in a heap of toile at Simone's feet.

"We will be speaking to the Paradigms about this," my mother assures the concierge.

"Better it happened at the end of the reception," Nigel says.

We return to the ballroom where the guests gather their bags, finish glasses of wine, divvy up centerpieces. The destruction is precise, as if performed with a scalpel, so succinct it is easily avoidable, many of the guests not even aware of the chaos.

"I don't think Granny likes your husband," Simone says. She steadies herself with one hand pressed against my side. We laugh until tears form.

It is almost time to pull the pashmina over the shoulders of the night and go home. My stepfather attempts to lead my mother away, but her gaze is fixed on Simone. Already concerned over the late addition, she's become a detective. Our laughter has hit her in the mother place where no one can hide. "We haven't been introduced," she says. "Who are you?"

"Simone," Simone says.

"He's so brave, isn't he?" Aunt Henshaw says. "I'm saying *he* because she's not a woman. It's very big these days."

"Who's not a woman?" my mother says.

My mother-in-law realizes first. "Your sister," she says.

"What sister?" my mother says. "She doesn't have a . . ."

Simone does not flinch or cower. "Me, Mother."

My mother's cheeks purple as she mentally passes through several understandings, none of them gracious. "I should have guessed." She bats away my stepfather's grip. "Are you here to ruin the day?"

"I can't be held responsible for an old inn's flimsy infrastructure, Mother."

"I can ruin things myself," I say. "I don't need anyone's help."

"It can't be Tom," my mother says to no one.

"It's not," I say. "It's Simone."

"A woman," my mother says. My stepfather attempts to collect her in his arms. My mother-in-law leers nearby, aunts and uncles hinging behind her. My mother's gaze flicks from us to them, aware that her reaction will be public. This could signal illness or collapse. She's going to fart, I worry. What she does is more putrid. She stretches out her arms, to lift onto the crucifix, but no, she signals to us, Simone and me, to enter into the area she has created, which seems to be (it cannot be) an embrace. "Yes," she says. "Yes." Simone and I watch as she performs magnanimity. We can handle honest revulsion but not showy liberalism. "My

daughters," she says. The crowd looks to us for reaction. Mother
has become a bird with one consistent call: *Yes.* As if she's been
reading dollar-store self-help. She has found radical acceptance
under the awning of others' points of view. "Yes!" the bird cries,
advancing. "I say yes." Because we will not meet it she brings the
hug to us, she will suffocate us with her open-mindedness to
make this public point.

"No," Simone says, for both of us.

The deejay's amplified voice informs everyone that the evening's embers are growing faint, that they might feel immortal,
numb with food, and dim with wine, but time is finite and it's
best to gather one's things and tell those you hate that you hate
them before we die. What she actually says is, "Last chance for
romance," and plays a final song.

"Water damage," the concierge proclaims, emerging from
a side door. "Someone must have been smoking and set off a
sprinkler. Water leaked into the floor." Who would do that and
not tell anyone, everyone wonders.

Simone and I are alone with our mother whose tone shifts to
reflect granite's compassion. "You haven't changed into anything
new," my mother says to Simone. "You still ruin everything."

"There you are, Mother. I thought we lost you." Strength ignites in Simone's eyes. "You're still a cold bag."

My mother is so confused she's grinning. "You're calling me
a bag but you're a degenerate." The word falls amid the remnants
of spangles and batting and gum and lemon basil and punctured
flooring.

In the end, the deejay is the most important person at the
wedding because she has the honor of declaring it kaput. Guests
not staying at the Inn want to make good time getting home. Carrying wrapped cake slices, overcoats, returned Tupperware from

other parties, damaging shoes, shouldering centerpieces, each other's purses, tired Rodrigo, ditzy with icing, stressed by the thought of driving, doing their best, the guests we've received and abandoned, received and abandoned, recto verso, stream by like river fish as we dismiss them one last time (goodbye, goodbye, goodbye) from the broken dance floor.

SIMONE LOOKS AT THE LAKE

The wedding party and Simone follow the crowd to the lobby. Panic slips through me as we reach the front door that on any other night I'd assume would lead outside. I worry this wedding will not let me pass, though every moment a guest pushes through and is enveloped by whatever's out there. Things like dream logic don't happen to the groom. He glides through the doorway and we are outside. I inhale the salve of night. Cars shine darkly in the parking lot. Party shoes make pleasant taps on the asphalt. You see only parts of people on nights like this. The crescent moon of a calf retracting into a sedan. A pale arm, reaching out to steady a lover. The star of a cheek held out for a farewell kiss. The cover-ups each person has chosen in a color that corresponds to their clothing make my heart feel scraped. Faces of those starting their cars, lit by the consoles, scattered bulbs in the darkness.

The wedding is over. Relief makes me an empathic daughter. I find my mother in the crowd. "Mother," I say. "Thank you for your help with the wedding. This must be a shock, and I hope that one day you will accept Simone for who she is."

"It's such a shame." Her expression is flat. "We paid so much for that dress."

She and my stepfather walk into the parking lot until they, too, fade into parts, the cornflower shawl, the wink of her satin heels. Her face momentarily lit by the car's center console, then extinguished. Like Ewan McGregor, my mother finds herself, when on the precipice of connection, lacking. I no longer fault her. It's not easy in there.

All the while the lake has been watching, gems marveling on its surface. Idling in its depths. The lake is now famous to me. I will compare every other lake to it, forever.

In the farthest dark, sitting in her car, Simone looks at the lake. Her profile against the water's light is placid and intimate. By observing we are intruding.

"What's he doing?" the groom says.

"She's looking at the lake," I say. "It's a perfectly fine thing to do."

His mouth opens into a grin he assumes is harmless. "So. Your brother is a woman now? The world is a fucked-up place."

"It is," I say. "But this is not an example of that."

He remembers a check he was supposed to give to the deejay and returns inside. Moonlight turns my skin quartz. I watch my sister look at the lake.

I think of the photograph Rose showed me of Santa Cruz. Friendly hedges growing alongside the driveways. The affirmation of hills in the distance. In my life I've had two profound realizations of the obvious. Arriving at inconvenient times, they showed me nothing I hadn't known, but in a new way that forced me to see how foolish or reckless I'd become and would not permit anything other than reversal. I can't say why in this moment the image of Santa Cruz houses occurs to me and I am overtaken by this simple fact: Every evening in California, the sun sets. The glint careening off ocean snarl, the intense business of acacias, branches blurred gold. A child seated on a driveway tossing a toy to herself. I see it as if projected onto a screen, with the nostalgia possessed only by people who've never visited a place. And then I have another realization, this one simpler: I must restart some forgotten engine and perform a grand re-steering, and this decision will hurt many people. A new light settles over me, a reprise of one I'd forgotten. I see every shivering pair of bare shoulders in the lot where I watch my sister stare at a lake and wait for a man who is fine, awakened by a photograph of Santa Cruz ranch-style homes. Another life. A part of me tosses to myself and is caught. I know what I want: to sit at the bar of a restaurant running a straw through an interesting drink waiting for a friend I'm looking forward to talking to and not be married to anyone.

"I knew it," all the bridesmaids say, sighing on a worn couch in my mind. "She didn't seem excited."

In the lobby, a few of our guests amble out of the mercurial elevator. They announce that they will have a drink at the bar and it would be unthinkable for the groom and me not to join them. The groom returns and accepts the offer for both of us.

"I want to speak with you," I tell him. But he says it'd be rude not to accept.

We file into the Inn's bar.

"Did you have fun?" one of the women asks. "Was it the best?"

"The best," I say. To the groom: "We need to talk right now."

"We have our whole lives to talk," he says. The wedding has made him so likable he's trying out comedy bits. Amid their fits of laughter I slip outside. Simone's car is there but she is gone. Is she swimming? Trudging through the woods? Now that she is back in my life even a short absence is an enemy to me, whereas other people could be missing for years and barely produce an emotional stir. I want to talk to her more than I want peaceful old age. A cousin returns from retrieving a bag from her car.

"There she is." She gasps, several yards away. "The bride."

A ROOM AFTER A ROOM

When the groom wakes I am standing over him, wearing my shoes and coat. I have already thrown up into the toilet and brushed my teeth. His naked chest and mussed hair makes me feel extra clothed.

"We made a mistake," I say. "It's not pretty but it's true."

He leaves the room and I follow. In the kitchenette he pours two glasses of dirt-colored liquid. He hands me one then sits on the opposite couch, takes a large sip. "Define mistake," he says.

I've already had the conversation five times in my head and am frustrated in advance of him not understanding. "As in, something we shouldn't have done."

"Why should we not have done it?" His words are exaggerated, patient. He speaks to a frustrating but well-intentioned child.

"I think you'd agree we've been drifting apart for a long time. We haven't had sex in over a year."

"Two nights ago," he says, and I say, "Before that."

"You told me you weren't a sexual person."

During a previous argument, I lied and said I wasn't sexual to avoid the truth that would create a one-way gate. But now I must see whether he is a front for something more compelling or if he is plaster that rejects the drill, and underneath is more exterior, and underneath more exterior.

I take a large sip. "I am a sexual person," I say.

"No." He is confused. "You're not. Didn't therapy help you understand that you are not a sexual person because of your injury?"

"Which injury?" I say.

His voice contains barely managed frustration. "Which? Injury?"

"It's fair to say I have issues, but it's also fair to say that you do, too."

He straightens. "I think we can both agree that I am a sexual person."

This brag stings, but I must permit micro-cruelties and remain perfect in this lightning field because I dragged the flawed measure of our relationship out on the day after our wedding.

"It's no one's fault," I say. "It's about the heat we conduct when we're together. Or lack thereof."

"Or lack thereof?"

"I think so," I say. "Yes."

He switches his crossed leg from left to right. "Scoreboard," he says. "One, you don't initiate physical intercourse with me. Two, you don't wear suggestive clothing. You don't even like to watch porn." He notices the effect this accusation has on me and changes tack. "But let's take your word that you are a sexual person. This is good news. We can add this essential part into our relationship. And there goes your lack thereof." He smiles, triumph.

"There's still a lack thereof," I say.

"Tell me more." The request sounds so tender I think I will be able to explain in a way he will understand.

"The truth is, I am a sexual person. I'm just not sexually attracted to you."

He taps his fingers against the glass, which contains either two sips or one strong one, wipes the condensation against his thigh. "Why are you bringing this up the day after we're married?"

"I've been on mute," I say.

He has tolerated this discussion as long as he plans to. "Is this about your client?" He places a stink on the word.

"This is not about my client," I say, redeeming the word.

His lip curls around a cruel remark. "I think you should take a fucking walk." The room bristles then settles. It is as if every object—the melancholic lamps, the belittling mini-soaps, the rigid carpet—has chosen his side.

"A walk might be a good idea. Clear my head."

In the bedroom I chuck my belongings into my suitcase. Eyeglasses, pajamas. I can't think of anything I would mind never seeing again. Make it appear spur-of-the-moment, I remind myself. Cheer bubbles in me when I think of sleeping alone, which pinks my ears with shame. I return to the room. If he finds a discrepancy between the idea of a walk and the packed suitcase, he doesn't mention it. Cheer and shame.

"You're really doing this." He never had to work hard to be admitted into good schools, teams, groups, associations. I am the only bad thing that's ever happened to him.

"I love you." His tone contains the punctured tenderness that could on any other morning strip my resolve. "I married you." He places his head in his hands, tears filling his eyes. "Please don't. Stay. I've been good to you."

"You have, kind of." I leave. Between the hotel room door and the elevator is the longest hallway in the world.

DO NOT SHELVE ITEMS IN AISLE THREE WITHOUT ASKING JOANNA

"Checking out?" the concierge says.

"I am but my husband is staying." I slide my key over the counter. She does not register anything amiss about the statement or my behavior, a kindness she has maintained throughout my stay. "Thank you for this week," I say. "I'll remember it always."

"I'll say." Her eyebrows ascend with amusement. "I'll remember you, the bride who got stuck in the elevator."

"And fell through the floor," I say.

"And the floor." She nods.

"I will remember this inn . . ." But my thinking halts. Fondly? As the site of my life's most baffling week? In the end I can't decide and leave the remark unfinished, *I will remember this Inn . . .* and exit the glass door within this ellipsis.

On the front landing I reposition my bag's strap to a more amenable place on my shoulder. This seems to signal to the car idling at the farthest part of the lot to turn itself on and drive toward me. Seagulls fan out over the lake. It's a regular morning for so many people, I think, watching Simone approach. I've blown up my life and left a good man. I feel scaled. Bereft. Dangerous. Joyful.

My phone rings.

"You are a terrible person," the groom's mother says. "And I always knew it. Disgusting. Brown gypsy scarper." She pauses for response and when there is none, continues. "There's something wrong with you. I knew the second I met you."

It doesn't seem possible the groom has already called her and explained everything, but I can no longer assume I have a firm grasp on time.

The car pulls up and brakes as the groom's mother lists my faults. I am a finicky flake who ruins the work good people do.

Simone wears cocktail party makeup. Eggplant lipstick. A crisp scarf is knotted against her throat. Her driving gloves calm me.

"You owe us money," the groom's mother says.

I tell her to let me know the amount and I will write a check. "There is something wrong with me," I say.

This pleases her. "Very wrong," she corrects.

"Very, very wrong," I suggest.

"Maybe you two could work it out." She reconsiders. "You're not unreasonable."

"That won't be possible." Simone pops the trunk. I place my suitcase inside and hang up.

"That was the groom's mother," I say, climbing in. "I am not a good person."

"Are you saying that or did she?"

"She did but maybe I'm saying it, too."

"I hope you told her to shove it." She glances over. "You didn't. I would have." Simone pulls the car away from the entrance. "What is a good person? I've never been able to figure it out."

"Depends who you ask," I say, and she says, "Exactly. So you better be careful who you ask."

Simone points to the lake. "I saw a sailboat," she says. "Right before you came out."

"It's too cold for sailboats."

"Not everyone hates the cold like you do. Maybe they're testing for next season. That happens. They have to test."

"Where?" I say.

She pulls the car to the water's edge and brakes. "There. It went into one of those inlets. It'll be back out in a second. Red with an orange stripe. I swear."

No one rushes out of the Inn to chase me. No one sits in the cars surrounding us. The lot is empty.

"Hey." She reacts to my doubt. "Good things still happen."

I place my hand next to hers though we don't touch. This is my soul, I think. And this is Simone's. "I'm glad you didn't die," I say. "That time."

"Thank you." She pulls out her phone. "I'm going to take a picture of that boat. You'll see. This lake is stunning. No wonder everyone's always talking about it." She's giddy. "Let's take a picture together. Like this." She holds her phone in front of us and I slide closer. Her crispness. Her warmth. She counts, takes it. "Shall we put it on your account?"

"Mine's not very . . ." I draw it up on my phone and show her. One picture of a tree at dusk.

She looks at me with pity. "It's like you're not even in the world. We'll use my dummy account." She scrolls so I can see: forests, houses, city corners, flashes of Adrian. A sign: DO NOT SHELVE ITEMS IN AISLE THREE WITHOUT ASKING JOANNA.

"I've seen that before," I tell her. "But I can't remember where."

"It's from my neighborhood grocery store," she says. "Who does Joanna think she is? It makes me want to shelve items to spite her. There," she says. "You're added."

We wait by the water. The unseasonably warm weather has delayed the changing of the leaves. Only one tree in the parking lot is going for it.

"It will be Thanksgiving soon," I say.

"Do you still celebrate that colonialist nonsense?" she says.

"I do," I admit.

"I do, too."

"Well then," I say. "We're married."

When I say I realized the sun goes down in California and that this triggered a vaulting from my life, I don't mean a photograph was the reason. It was only the last in a series.

I broke a towel rack after an unrepeatable set of events. I re-glued it but after a week it fell again. The old glue built into a deposit that changed the shape of the holding part. Reinjury is worse than injury. We tell ourselves stories about ourselves to try to crack the old glue off. Lord knows if the new part will hold.

"Let's list everyone we think should shove it," Simone says. "I'll start," she says. "Mom."

Through the dull perches of time and too long since that surge of awakening, on the nights we are certain of the unbearable wrongness of coexistence, the birds get in. Tiny, inconsequential shifts put me in a new position from which I could see unexpected vistas or be approached by unlikely people. One shift leads to another as you make room for yourself again and again. I readjusted several times over the course of years to allow myself to arrive.

I'VE BEEN MARRIED
HUNDREDS OF TIMES

If I were to subject myself to that which I subject others, and build a diorama of my life, I'd place a petite, ethnically ambiguous woman at a table in a red kitchen. It would be summer, her favorite season, yet she'd be wearing jeans because she's ashamed of the plum-colored scarring that maps her right side. It would be her grandmother's kitchen, on the table a miniature box of gingersnaps and a pair of binoculars used to spy on the neighbors. If I were ambitious, I'd string wire from the outside gutter to a plastic tree, and on it I'd place a few judgmental budgies whose bright colors don't belong in New York's palette. The woman's conversation partner, her grandmother, would be a realistically rendered parakeet, because there can be no accurate representation of my life that doesn't include an element of oddity that has always been a border between me and the "right-minded" world in which women walk down aisles experiencing simple happinesses. I'd build the bird myself, every gentle feather.

People who know me now don't know I was ever married, or estranged from my sister. I think about my wedding on nights I

want to remind myself of myself. Life has no past tense: To remember something is to relive it. I'm smiling at my sister and
I'm also lying prone in the ambulance covered in a thin sheet.
I'm watching a woman mail her shoes. I'm with my grandmother
in the antechamber. I'm breathing on a bench in Union Square,
helping Danny overturn cushions to find the remote on an endless, unremarkable day. My great-grandmother is always curling
her hair, gazing over the roiling sea. The parakeets are always
blinking into the cracked sunlight and realizing, this is somewhere much harder than Argentina. The street dancer is always
looking over her remarkable shoulder. I am always lying on that
floor in shared blood, reaching toward Yuna in her last moments
and finding myself, as I always do when in fingertip's distance of
connection, lacking.

I'd need dioramas for these watershed moments, too, and when
presenting my life to the governing body, I'd say: To understand
this woman you must know that each is happening simultaneously.

I'm always sitting in the parked car the day my sister, Simone,
drives me away from my life, waiting for a sailboat, making a list
of people who can shove it.

"Rodrigo," I say. "Flagels. Long Island."

"Christ yes," she says. "Do you know they say *on* Long Island?
As in, you are on this piece-of-garbage island and it's going to be
for a long time."

"Above Long Island," I say. "Outside."

"Long Island can shove itself on and up its own ass."

"You really hate this island. Who broke up with you who was
from here?"

She smiles. "I broke up with her."

I've grown up with the woman sitting next to me, but I don't
know whether she prefers winter to summer, hates root veg-

etables, if she gets cold easily. If she's one of those people who regularly has an unseen hair hanging in front of her eyes she can never grab. I like being nowhere near figuring her out.

"Why didn't Granny leave me alone after I found you?" I say. "I did what she asked."

"Who knows with that woman?" She refreshes her lip gloss in the rearview mirror. "Maybe you didn't do it fast enough, or the way she wanted. Maybe she knew she could count on me to bring the whole enterprise crashing down."

"Where is the sailboat I've been promised?" I say.

"It'll be here," Simone says. "Wait."

It's true what Rose said about happiness. But it wasn't that I thought I didn't deserve it, it's that I don't consider her idea happiness. Happiness was only ever on its way as I waited in the peony room, the elevator, the grocery store. When I hear my sister on the line or see her driving gloves, mint colored with roses at the wrist, I am met. When the ship hits, I chase it.

"It's probably going to take a while to settle everything," I say. "Apartment. Car."

"I can't imagine a thing a woman can go through that can't be beautiful."

"You do ruin everything."

She says, "Family trait."

Simone and I have time and working arms and legs and are in good moods. I lean forward to see out from under the windshield where she points.

"How do you be a bride?" I asked the hairdresser on the morning of my wedding. "This is the first time I've been one."

I meant, how does one join oneself to another? Thinking of it now, there are many ways. Renting space within my mother, Rose turning at the sound of her name, listening to my sister's tender voice. There are intimacies that don't involve marriage just as there are marriages that don't involve intimacy. The mind provides the only possible privacy so what is more intimate than thought? If intimacy is marriage, I'm married to anyone I've carried in my mind. If intimacy is marriage, I've felt more married to the EMT who could have left but instead pressed her palm against my heart for the length of several breaths to make sure I was still tethered to the world. That EMT married me, if you will. Will you? If you say I do, these are vows. Will you stay if I change into something you couldn't anticipate and don't recognize? Will you be honest with me when I'm present, about me when I'm absent? Will you encourage me to be as much like myself as possible? Will you hide what I use to cause pain? The drugs, the credit card, the words. Will you take my picture in front of every tree I like from now until . . . ? Will you not only look at but delight in what I point to? Look at this sailboat, look at the moon at its brashest, the parakeet, activating out of the dusk. Every day from now until ellipsis? Again? Until? Again? Say yes and we are married. If intimacy is marriage, every time you are my first thought upon waking we marry again.

Simone slips her hand into mine, a simple movement like an afterthought. We peer at the body of water, waiting for something to arrive, willing to believe that whatever does can be good. I hold my sister's hand, a small, precious bird.

ACKNOWLEDGMENTS

For their care with the author and/or the manuscript of *Parakeet*, a universe of gratitude to:

Claudia Ballard, my agent and hero; the Munster Literature Centre; University College Cork, Cork City; the Sewanee Writers' Conference; the MacDowell Colony; Hedgebrook Writers in Residence program; the Center for Fiction; Institute of American Indian Arts; New York University; the New School; *One Story*; *Catapult*; University of Iowa Press; Mira Jacob, Lauren Groff, and Laura van den Berg for gifting their early, lovely words; Lydia Zoells and the team at Farrar, Straus and Giroux; and my wise editor, Jenna Johnson.

Tanya Rey, Phyllis Trout and Brian Brooks, Elliott Holt, Halimah Marcus, Steph Opitz, Grace Lavery, Angel Nafis and Shira Erlichman, Manuel Gonzales, Ramona Ausubel, Christine Vines, Derek Palacio, Anne Ray, Shawn-Aileen Clark, Claire Vaye Watkins, Téa Obreht and Dan Sheehan, Charles Hagerty and Pip Pickering, Thomas Morris, Thomas Grattan, Yuka Igarashi, Julia Strayer, the Dodson family, and my students, who help me stay in love with "what every second goes away" (Ross Gay).

Helene Bertino, who allows for me. Adina Talve-Goodman, Mr. Fox, and Sophie, who I carry.

A NOTE ABOUT THE AUTHOR

Marie-Helene Bertino is the author of *2 A.M. at The Cat's Pajamas* and the story collection *Safe as Houses*. She was the 2017 Frank O'Connor International Short Story Fellow in Cork, Ireland. Her work has received the O. Henry Award, the Pushcart Prize, the Iowa Short Fiction Award, and the Mississippi Review Prize, and has twice been featured on NPR's *Selected Shorts*. She has been awarded fellowships from the MacDowell Colony, the Sewanee Writers' Conference, and the Center for Fiction. Formerly an editor at *One Story* and *Catapult*, she now teaches at NYU, the New School, and the Institute of American Indian Arts in Santa Fe. In spring 2020, she was the Kittredge Distinguished Visiting Writer in the MFA program at the University of Montana. Visit her website at www.mariehelenebertino.com.